FELL OF

DARK

FELL

OF

DARK

A Novel

Patrick Downes

PHILOMEL BOOKS

An Imprint of Penguin Group (USA)

PHILOMEL BOOKS
Published by the Penguin Group
Penguin Group (USA) LLC
375 Hudson Street, New York, NY 10014

USA | Canada | UK | Ireland | Australia | New Zealand | India | South Africa | China
penguin.com   A Penguin Random House Company

Library of Congress Cataloging-in-Publication Data
Downes, Patrick, 1968–
Fell of dark : a novel / Patrick Downes.
pages cm
Summary: Chronicles the lives of two mentally ill boys—Erik, who believes he
is a saint, and Thorn, who believes he is a demon—as their minds devolve into
hallucinations, showing the way their worlds intersect, and culminating in a
final stand-off.
[1. Mental illness—Fiction. 2. Good and evil—Fiction. 3. Hallucinations and illu-
sions—Fiction.] I. Title.
PZ7.1.D687Fel 2015
[Fic]—dc23
2014037606

Printed in the United States of America.
ISBN 978-0-399-17290-8
10 9 8 7 6 5 4 3 2 1

Edited by Jill Santopolo. Design by Siobhán Gallagher.
Text set in 11-point Photina MT Std and 10.25-point Caslon 3 LT Std.
The publisher does not have any control over and does not assume any re-
sponsibility for third-party websites or their content.

FOURTEEN

Miracles are not contrary to nature,
but only contrary to what we know about nature.

—Saint Augustine, *The City of God*, Book XXI

ERIK

Eulogy

IT'S ALL I KNOW how to do, all I've ever done: read and think and write. I have to write to someone. That someone is you.

I've known you since before we were born. Aren't all true loves, the really great loves, destined? All we have to do is meet. When will I learn your name?

Go ahead, ask me a question. When was I first hurt? When did I first see you? When did the first miracle happen? When was my first kiss? When did I first write a eulogy?

Eulogy for a Young Boy

He thought. He wrote. He read. He ran and drank milk. A boy made of milk and concrete. He was cut in two. He bled. He died.

A stranger smart enough to steal a child and lock a door took the boy's life. The man cut him in half, then chewed him up. Blood and rubble.

Even though the boy was dead, he dreamed up a girl with skin and hair of light, taking care of him, holding his hand. He dreamed the girl

gave him a kiss, and he wondered if the kiss
would send him back to the world. It didn't. It
kept him under. He sleeps in the box with the
girl made from light.

We have to forget him so we can take him
with us.

That's the eulogy exactly as it came out of me a little less than
six months ago, the day I turned fourteen. I haven't touched it.
I've read it a few dozen times, and I still can't be sure I understand it. But I can tell you this: I had died. I eulogized myself.

I remember the locked garage and screaming for it to be un-
locked. I remember a square of brown sunlight on the floor of
the garage and a window I couldn't reach. Why couldn't I figure how to reach the window? Why couldn't I stack crates and
climb out? I could've broken the glass and escaped. I don't know.
I can't exactly tell you what happened in that garage, except I
left it without the belt I had to hold up my pants, my zipper was
broken, and I was bleeding. My right arm didn't look like mine.

I don't remember what happened, or how many times I
ended up in that garage. It might've been once or a thousand
times, but I died, and this came so soon after my mother lost
my father.

No, she didn't lose him, like he was a mitten or a penny
dropped through a hole in her pocket. A car killed him in the
street.

2

Half-Orphan

MY FATHER'S NAME WAS Ian Lynch, and he died right before I turned five. I don't remember much about him. I remember he rubbed his beard on my neck and called it a goat's kiss. I remember he limped as if he dragged an invisible chain behind him. Walking made his legs ache, so he preferred to ride his bicycle. I remember he sometimes carried me in the metal basket clamped to the front of the bike. I loved the wind and bumpy streets.

I remember the morning he died. I was crouching by my bed with my head between my knees, watching a beetle crawl around the floor. How much can a beetle carry? I wanted to know, so I pressed my thumb into its back. The beetle stopped. Even when I picked up my thumb, the beetle stayed put. Then I crushed the beetle. Why? I don't know. I don't know now any more than I knew then. The crack of its body, like a nutshell, scared me. A milky liquid bubbled up from its broken back.

"Erik?"

My mother came running across the apartment. Did she hear the beetle break? I kicked it under my bed.

"Erik, come on with me."

My mother took my arm and pulled me hard behind her. That's when I started to cry and told her I killed the beetle.

We took a taxi to the hospital. We didn't really have money for the luxury of a taxi, so this meant something serious. My mother couldn't talk to me. She cried. I watched her. Her shoulders shook, and her nose leaked over the knuckles of her hand.

The cabby pulled up to the curb. "Emergency, right?" In the rearview mirror, he had only one eye, off-center.

My mother nodded and opened her purse.

"Keep your money," the driver said. "I never take money outside Emergency."

We waited at reception, holding hands. I heard the voices of panic and work, my mother's voice and the receptionist's. Voices without bodies. A typewriter. The wheel of a bed. Shoes on the floor, squeak, squeak; a rubber stamp; a revolving door, thwup, thwup; the bell of an elevator.

There were all these sounds, and then one more. A crumpled-up girl strapped into a wheelchair. She was a crushed beetle. And she was a kettle, steam coming out of her ears and a long, high whistle.

A nurse wearing a uniform as bright as the walls took my hand and led me away from my mother and the girl. She offered me a lollipop and asked me my name. I didn't understand what was happening. My mother held her face in her hands, and a doctor spoke to her. He was dressed in white, his stethoscope around his neck and his eyes on his shoes. The girl in the wheelchair had disappeared. My father had already been dead two hours.

My father died. A week or a month later, I was locked in a garage, and then the headaches came. I'd hear trains in my head. I heard them like we lived in the middle of Grand Central Station under the ceiling of painted stars, where trains meet and talk and say good-bye, and I'd ask my mother, "Do you hear the trains, Mama? Hear them?"

My mother would say, "No, Erik. I don't hear any trains."

A little while later, the trains would hit me, and I would be in too much pain even to scream, and my mother would try to get me to lie still, but with each train, I would feel the impact and throw myself against the wall or onto the floor, and there was the pain in my head until the trains left the station.

Silence.

Everything gone from inside my head. Only long, rumbling echoes and the ringing tracks.

Mother

MY FATHER DIED ALMOST nine years ago, and my mother hasn't slept a night in what was their bed. I've seen her slumped on the couch, but usually, almost always, she sleeps in an armchair. Not a reclining armchair either. She piles blankets on top of her and falls asleep half sitting, her legs propped on the ottoman; a crossword puzzle, a pair of reading glasses, and a fine-point felt-tip pen on her lap. Sometimes a nail file. Sometimes sections of a newspaper. Sometimes her checkbook propped open by her finger. Most often a crossword. She sleeps with her face lit by the floor lamp shining down over her shoulder.

Whenever I see her like this, I feel sorry for her and for myself. I feel sorry for her because I can't ever believe she's comfortable or sleeping well. Sorry for myself because I've never been a good enough son, even with the miracles, to persuade her, just once in nine years, to sleep lying down.

I know my mother is a mother when I walk by her in the middle of the night. I might bump into the ottoman or ripple the air enough by my quietest step, and she'll come to the surface with a nervous question.

"Are you all right?"

"Can I get you something?"

"Do you have a headache?"

Only a mother would wake up like this. Or only a widowed mother.

I'll stand over her for a while looking at her face. My mother. She's right-handed, and when she drinks tea, she holds her left hand to her chest, cupped, like she's protecting an invisible bird. For her, my father's death was a wound that never healed.

I ask her, "Do you want me to turn off the light?"

In a defenseless voice, sounding much younger than me, she'll say, "Yes, please," or, "No, thank you, leave it on." When she asks me to leave the light on, I wonder about what hall in her memory would go black without that floor lamp shining right into her face.

There are times when she'll barely wake and mumble. I can't make it out. It's her dreaming language. I'm convinced she's trying to ask me if I'm all right even as she's flying or fighting a troll with a sword.

The worst, though, the very worst, is when she wakes up and says, "I'm sorry." She must be talking to my father.

Last night, I went to the kitchen for a drink, and my mother asked if I had a headache. I told her no, but I did have a headache. It woke me up. I knew snow was coming. After a long time, I went back to sleep. I looked out this morning, and three inches had fallen. The snow kept coming. My head felt better. Sometimes, the headaches are as simple as that.

◇

My mother belongs to the sisterhood of beautiful women. If I didn't believe in some kind of god, I'd think a committee, the Committee of Appearance, discussed her over a lunch of cocktails. They got drunk and dreamed up one of those women who comes along every hundred or thousand years. Luckily, one voice of reason kept the committee from being totally merciless. She doesn't have dimples, and she has a hole in her heart.

They returned to their office, the Committee of Appearance, down the hall from the Committee on Death and Disintegration, and put their heads on their desks and forgot what they'd done.

Her eyes are two diamonds, glittering, honest, and almost impossible to look at with the naked eye. Even I find it hard.

I do believe in a god, though, and I have to think my mother shows His sense of humor and mercy.

One day, I know, your beauty will blow me apart. You will have no mercy at all.

My mother has a plum-colored mouth. Her skin is soft and cool and blue. Have you ever held a woman as thin and purple as a blade of strange grass? As fragile as that? My mother, when I hug her, moans a little, which means she feels good.

When I was young, my mother brushed through her straight black hair every morning. Her hair hung down to her waist back then. Once, when my father was already gone, though I didn't know that meant forever, she twisted her hair into a rope for me to hold. I couldn't get my hands around it, and all her hair slipped out. Oranges. I smelled oranges.

"Darling," she said. Then, she handed me her hairbrush and put her hands in her lap. "You've watched me a hundred times. You know what to do."

The silver brush was one of my mother's heirlooms. It was her mother's, and it felt heavy in my hand. I heard the sound of the bristles in her hair, like papery wings. Butterflies flew up out of her hair.

"Does Daddy brush your hair?"

"No," she sighed. "His hands were too big and clumsy. You're doing wonderfully, sweetheart."

I felt proud, and my mother reached behind to pat my leg.

"Mama, can you have two husbands?" My mother laughed. "Can you?"

"Why do you ask?"

I couldn't answer, and she turned to face me. All that beauty.

"Erik, my son, my only son." She held my chin and kissed my forehead.

My mother could never be my wife, but she would be my first love all the same.

First Miracle

LAST NIGHT, I WENT to sleep with a headache, and I had a dream you rode up to me on a bicycle. I couldn't make out your face, but I knew it was you. Your bicycle was like my father's, except your basket was more girly, woven out of willow or something. You put your hands on my head and said, "I wish I could take away the pain."

"You could make it snow," I said, "or get me a new head."

You laughed, and the snow came.

Sometimes, I've gotten other people confused with you, like my first-grade teacher, Mrs. Quist. I loved her, but I was six, and she was twenty-six when we met. She told me her age in the hallway outside the teachers' lounge.

Older boys from the school, sixth graders, or Mr. Jimson, the science teacher, would come to her classroom to visit her or offer to help with anything she might need. She always said no to them, but never meanly. Just no-thank-you. This one morning, she tried to take too much in her hands, and I had been hanging back watching her, pretending to fix a book cover or something, and she simply couldn't make it all work out.

I said, "Can I help, Mrs. Quist?"

She seemed surprised to see me there at all, like I was a two-headed cow. Then she looked relieved. "Yes, Erik. Would you please carry these books and follow me to the teachers' lounge?" I remember a little gold pendant with a green stone, and she had on perfume.

I walked next to her, carrying her books, listening to her heels strike the hall floor, and at least one older boy stared out from the walls. For conversation, I said, "How old are you, Mrs. Quist?"

"Twenty-six," she said, "but never ask a woman her age, Erik. I might not have answered if I were thirty. I might've gotten annoyed."

"How old is Mr. Quist?"

"Thirty-four."

We were almost to the teacher's lounge. I don't know what got in my head, but I said, "Would you be sad if he died?"

Mrs. Quist stopped short. She looked down at me, and I could tell she didn't know what to say. She didn't look angry, just confused. She kneeled down, and I said, "Would you?"

"Erik." She took the books from my hands. "I don't know how you know what you know, but you do. I can see that."

"You're not happy."

She kneeled there, staring at her shoes or mine, I couldn't tell, and then she stood up. "You go and play."

This wasn't the miracle. There are sad women everywhere. I see it.

No. Mrs. Quist might have loved me because I could think and

11

read and write and talk and play music and sing and run and do my math homework without any help. Mrs. Quist might have loved the six-year-old boy she hoped to have for herself in her own son. Or maybe she saw in me a man she couldn't wait to see fully grown and would know she had some part in making.

Mrs. Quist loved me, I know it, and after our exchange outside the teachers' lounge, her attitude toward me changed a little. She looked at me almost shyly. She looked at me like she knew she couldn't hide her life and thoughts from me. She couldn't.

I loved her because she loved me.

Poor Mrs. Quist. The miracles started with her. Nothing complicated. I gave her a flower, and the flower never died. Simple.

It wasn't much of a flower at first. I picked a sickly white tulip from someone's yard and brought it to school for Mrs. Quist. I'll admit I spoke to the flower, whispered into the cup of petals, before I put it into a mug of water. The water was straight from the tap.

The flower got stronger in the water, and it wouldn't die.

When she first noticed it, Mrs. Quist said, "Thank you, somebody . . . Oh, Erik. A spring flower. The first tulip."

As it got stronger, she said, "Look how big and bright it is now. I didn't think that would happen at all. I should always expect a surprise from you, Mr. Lynch."

The last day of school, she stopped me before I left her class-room. "This flower won't ever die." She said it like that, not a question.

"No," I said. "Why would it?"

"I don't know," she said. "Because flowers die."

"You can kill it, but it won't die by itself."

Mrs. Quist rubbed a petal between her fingers. What could she have been thinking at that moment? She might have been frightened, confused, or sad. I don't know.

"I'll take it home with me and bring it back in September." She put her hand on my head, then on my shoulder. "You're some kind of boy."

Decision

I HAVEN'T SPOKEN AT all to anyone, you know, not even my mother, for three months.

Here are the reasons:

> The Rule of Benedict commanding silence
> Grief
> Anger
> Self-hatred
> Boredom
> Patience

Speak only when there's something worth saying. Speak only when it's necessary. When is there anything worth saying? Can you tell me? When is it necessary?

Grief for my mother, who might never get over her dead husband.

Angry I'm a teenager with no sense at all of what it is I'm supposed to do with my life. I have a few miracles, but they're just hints of something I can't know yet. Everything is hidden from me.

I don't understand the molester, the rapist, the murderer. I don't understand why my father had to be killed. I don't understand miracles. I don't understand headaches. I don't understand my friends and teachers. I don't understand violence, warfare, but I don't understand peace either. I don't understand God.

This is the real truth. I'm angry at God. I'm angry at God. But who isn't? Really, in our hearts, who isn't angry at God?

I hate myself for my anger. I feel it all the time, the ugly, inside. I hate myself because the inside ugliness makes me ugly on the outside. All that anger at God shows in my face like a bright, black light. Pure ugly.

I'm bored. Sloth, a deadly sin. I don't even have the energy to tell you why.

That's a joke.

What matters more, the measure of a side of a trapezoid or the measure of heaven? What matters more, the mystery of Boo Radley and Scout or the mystery of God and Lucifer?

I'm waiting on God. In my total silence, except for this testament, for your eyes only, I'm waiting on God. I wait for the slightest noise, a whisper.

Loss

THERE IS ONLY YOU. I lost all my other friends in the silence.

Nicolo, Nick, whose father is Edo and mother Italian, and who has blue eyes and an enormous Afro, and who all the girls fear and want.

Jerome, who can't stop stealing candy and burritos from the corner bodega, and throws a ball farther, jumps higher, and runs faster than almost anyone else I know. He might beat me by now, I don't know.

Holly, a tomboy, who's in love with Nick, though she doesn't know it yet, and who's started to give up baseball mitts to keep her hands soft. I'm just glad she still plays the trombone.

Martin the Irishman, who hit six feet two years ago and now has scraped past six five and weighs about 115 pounds. A hundred and fifteen pounds of pure gold. He stuck with me longest before he couldn't stand the weight of the quiet.

The last time I saw them all together was Martin's birthday party last October. He turned fourteen, and his mother invited me. I don't know why I went. I stood to one side and watched everything as if from behind a one-way mirror. I watched Nick slide away from one girl after another, because he's embarrassed by the attention when his closest friend, Martin, might never attract a girl. I saw Jerome balance on one foot and juggle two apples with one hand. There's nothing he can't do. Holly would look from Nick to me, like she wanted to come for advice.

Holly was angriest to lose me, and I miss her most. I love her. Not love love. I've never confused her with you. I mean love. Holly frowned at me, the way she might have frowned at something she neither saw nor heard but thought she had. Then she got her coat and left.

I followed her and caught up. I had a pen and paper with me and scribbled a note to her. *Be patient. Maybe not now, maybe not in a year, but you'll have your time with Nick.*

She read it and folded it into her pocket.

"You don't know how much I miss you, Erik. Why can't you just be normal and come back?"

I shrugged.

"Haven't you proved whatever it is you want to prove?"

I shook my head.

"Not even for me?" she said.

Another piece of paper, and the pen started dying. *I'm not trying to prove anything. I don't know what I'm supposed to say, and I don't want to hear my voice. A lot of reasons.*

"I don't understand," she said. "You'll lose everyone and everything."

Another Miracle

I REMEMBER THE FIRST time I thought of you. I was so sick, and I almost died from dehydration and a fever. I thought of you, invented you, I guess, and you bent down over me, and you kissed me, and I got better.

Warm milk and honey will help you sleep. My mother told me Mrs. Phoil, our neighbor, brought this over to help her sleep after my father died, and my mother gives it to me. It hasn't helped me yet. Not ever, I don't think.

"You never slept," my mother tells me. "Not even when I carried you. In me, in your crib, in your bed, you stayed awake, thinking, thinking, thinking. Not a moment's rest. We need sleep, Erik. Sleep keeps us sane."

I hardly ever remember feeling tired.

Now I'm not sleeping. I'm not sleeping because I have a terrible sore throat and a cough. I can't stop coughing. There are the remedies a person can buy in the drugstore. Then there are the ones people make up, like my mother's lemon, honey, ginger tea. Hot liquids of any kind, including chicken broth or soup. The most unusual I know about is this: a heaping teaspoon of black pepper and a teaspoon of honey mixed into a cup of milk, three times a day, won't fail to cure a cough.

Why do sore throats hurt so much? Nothing compares to my headaches, but a sore throat, the swollen gland under your jaw that, when you touch it, secretes pain, a sore throat—. I don't know. You don't want to put anything in your mouth. You don't want to talk in case a sharp letter stabs the tissue.

Five days I rolled around in a fever. It broke a day ago.

I'm sick of being sick. I think. I pray. I can't read, since my eyes are swirling in my head. Sometimes I feel as if I'm better, and I stand up only to feel weak, almost too weak to get to the bathroom.

Where's my mother? Working.

My mother works for the post office. She has a degree in fine art, and I know she would rather draw than talk, weigh envelopes, or give out stamps. We need to eat, so she does what she has to do. And the whole time, the public has to face Helen of Troy.

Kids stare at my mother. Dogs wag at her. Everyone, everyone looks at her, surprised, sometimes embarrassed, sometimes angry. Mostly, though, men look at my mother. She has a weirdly young, childlike expression, as pure as a doll's, like she's never suffered a thing in her life. Teenage boys not much older than me get confused and gawk at her, too, wondering if she might be close enough to them for love.

Also, and I hate to write this, everyone tells me she has a gorgeous body. She once nearly caused an accident when she bent over to tie her shoe. I was there. I saw the driver, a man, take his eyes off the road, forget himself, maybe wonder, as if he had all the time in the world in that split second, how a bird like my mother could have flown all the way from some secret forest on the other side of the planet, how she could've gotten so lost, and if he could ever, in a hundred lifetimes, capture her.

I used to ask my mother every day when she came home from work, "How many men tried to take you home today?"

"A couple."

"None."

"Too many to count."

"Oh, today, Erik, was a double-take day." This meant everyone seemed to need a couple chances to look at her before moving along.

"You'll see," she says. "You've got it, too. It comes from your grandmother."

My mother can't escape the attention. How many times could she have replaced my father if she wished? She might have married a lawyer or taken off with a surgeon.

My mother said, "I'm not for sale, Erik."

"What do you mean?" I said. I must have been ten.

"I mean a man can't think his checkbook will deliver me from the post office into his arms."

"It would make life easier."

"Yes. It would," she said. "Yes. But your father was a man I can't forget, and I like having you to myself."

"Why can't you forget Papa? I barely remember him."

"We had eight years together before you were born and thirteen before he died. We were young together. He had everything I wanted in a man, and I believed in him. We would've found our fortune together."

"We're poor," I said.

"No, not exactly poor. Just not well off. We have to earn, and we have to be careful."

"What about Mr. Munson down the block?"

"He's nice," she said.

"He drives that fancy car."

"You hardly care about money."

"I think you do."

"Be careful, Erik," she said. "I can't be bought. When the time comes, I'll open up to a man, date him, and you'll have a say. For now, like always, I think about your father. I hear him. I see him. I breathe him. Only him. Understand?"

By then, she was crying.

There was a time when I thought my mother fell in love with another man. A year and a half ago, in the summer. We visited her uncle who lives on the beach in Maine. It didn't take long before the usual herd started gathering around my mother. We'd go for ice cream, or to a movie, or to dinner at a lobster shack, and the teenage servers, girls or boys, would stare at her. She wore a bikini and denim shorts with her black hair, then just past her shoulders, pinned up, a few loose strands dangling

21

down her neck, sunglasses. I heard a woman tell her husband, "Just stop making it so obvious."

Her uncle, a confirmed bachelor who made a small fortune as a jingle writer, lived in semiretirement. I liked his friends. They all seemed funny, smart, good-looking, and laid-back. They were young and old. Some had kids my age, but not many.

One of these friends of his, Lincoln, worked in advertising, too, a writer. Tall, quiet, and funny in a way that goes right by you most of the time, he treated my mother respectfully. He never looked too deeply into her eyes, never put his hand on her hand or her shoulder, never tried to get to her through me, pretending he was my best friend. I knew he was what people call a gentleman, and I knew I wanted to be like him when I grew up.

Lincoln made my mother smile, and he seemed to make her feel a little nervous, a little giggly. He was a dark kind of handsome. He could make you laugh without laughing himself, or make you feel good without seeming to feel good or happy himself. He had an effect on my mother. You could see it. Sometimes she tried to avoid him, to walk to the other side of the room away from him, to look for an escape when he came in. It was like she couldn't trust herself around him. Like she might jump into his arms, or beg him to come home with us.

Lincoln was married.

Where was his wife? My mother didn't know. Her uncle wouldn't say.

Lincoln was married, and my mother left him alone for her own sake, and his, and mine. Maybe for his wife's, too.

It was Lincoln who was sitting on the deck the morning of a miracle.

At my great-uncle's, there's a wall I can jump off of and land on sand. I can climb it, too. One morning that summer, when I was twelve, I wanted to go swimming, and Lincoln Reynolds sat in a beach chair reading.

"Hello, Erik," he said. "Got plans?"

"Swimming."

"By yourself?"

"Yes."

He looked out over the water. "Sounds cold," he said. His book was closed in his lap, and he was marking the place with his finger. "Your mother's the most radiant woman," he started.

I nodded, and for a moment, I thought he was going to act like all the rest.

"I'm sorry," he said. "That was rude. Stupid." He glanced at me and smiled. "Go for your swim. I'll be right here, just in case."

When I got back from the ocean, swum out and cold, I climbed the wall and lay down on the wood deck. I was still wet.

"How was it?"

"Great."

"Not too cold?"

"No," I said. Then: "You're married, right?"

"Yes, I am."

"But you come here alone."

"Yes." He frowned at the ocean. "My wife loves the city and is no great fan of sand and surf."

"Do you have children?"

"No. Not yet."

"Do you wish you'd met my mother sooner?"

Lincoln laughed. He actually laughed. "Wow. One good turn," he said. "Yes, I do. A man would have to be out of his mind not to—." He interrupted himself and thought for a second. "I have no right to make any of us sad over it."

I said nothing. The sun dried me out, and I fell asleep with my arms straight out to the sides and my legs together, like I'd been crucified. This has always been comfortable for me. I woke up for lunch alone, Lincoln gone. When I got up, there was a water stain from my back on the boards of my uncle's deck. You could see me in the form of a cross in the wood. It was full sun, just about lunchtime, so I thought I'd watch the stain evaporate. I waited and waited. A year and a half later, there's still the image of my crucifixion in the deck.

Unrealistic Love

HERE'S A LETTER I wrote to you last year. Invisible you. It's not long.

> I know you were born today. I've never
> seen a winter day like this. January 20, and
> it hit 73 degrees in the park. Streets turned
> into streams of melted snow. The whole city
> splashed. The hot sun made strangers kiss, and
> the sad danced. Murderers and thieves slept. It's
> a Saturday, so I sat on a bench and watched the
> traffic lights turn red at the same time and the
> cars stop all at once. Everybody listened to the
> birds sing. *She's found her way in,* I thought. Now
> all we have to do is find each other. We will. Of
> course, we will.

Resolution

CHRISTMAS CAME AND WENT. Christmas Day, my mother and I ate in silence. When I cleared my throat, my mother dropped her fork on her plate and looked at me with such hope I felt ashamed. I thought: *Does my silence hurt her? Does the fact I haven't spoken to her stab her heart?*

I wanted to tell her, "You make the best turkey in the world." I wrote it on a piece of paper instead. My mother cried, and I had no right to beg her to stop.

For New Year's Eve, we ate pickled herring. I could eat a whole jar of herring. Actually, whatever you'd think to feed a seal would be good for me. Anything from the sea. I have small ears, and I sometimes bark like a seal, *ahr, ahr.*

I love you, I wrote my mother. *Happy New Year.*

"I love you, Erik, very much."

I waited, and then I wrote, *Mom, you're too sad.*

"You look so much like your father," she said.

Then listen to him.

"What's he saying?"

I don't know. Maybe he's saying, Magda, the next time a man asks you out to lunch, say yes.

"Is he?"

I'm sorry I wrote that.

"You don't communicate anything for so long, and then this?"

I'm sorry.

"You should be," she said. "You don't know how much I hurt, Erik. You don't know anything about it. You've never asked. You've been in your world. We've gotten by. I've gotten us by."

I nodded. I could feel my silence, my darkness. Why does anyone speak or write?

"The tricky thing is this," she said finally. "You're right. I'm dying on the vine."

I made resolutions yesterday. Here they are:

1. Write more, read more, think more
2. Volunteer at the soup kitchen at St. Barnabas
3. Try to get Mom to sleep in her bed
4. Stay alive

Pause

I WANT YOU TO hear the silence. I want you to breathe and listen. Let the gap represent all the things, unimportant and important, I've decided to keep to myself.

Kiss

MY MOTHER HAD TO rely on babysitters. No getting around it, a single mom. The one she used most, Janet Gill, began sitting for me when I was seven. Janet always wore dresses. That's how I remember it. Dresses no matter what the weather was like. She was five and a half years older than me and almost twice my height. At least it seemed like it. Most of her height was in her neck.

I remember the first time she made me feel like a giant.

She nearly laughed when I dragged her huge schoolbag into the apartment. My mother had raised me to be a gentleman. I carry bags when I can. I open doors. I stand when a woman enters the room. I offer my seat. I walk on the outside. So I brought in Janet's bag, and she said, "Let me feel your muscles, big boy." I must have blushed, because she smiled. I saw row after row of tiny bright teeth. "Come on, bashful, let me feel."

I made a muscle for her, curling my skinny arm. My body shook I tried so hard to make a muscle worth showing. I dreamed up muscles to impress her. Janet pinched my arm between her fingers and nodded once, a weird frown of approval. "You're a strong boy," she said. "It's like a little stone in there. Imagine what you'll be like when you're grown up."

I felt proud. Every time she came to the house, I wanted her to touch my arm, or my legs, or my shoulders and tell me I was strong. She touched me, and she smiled, and I became a giant to keep her company.

Finally, everything changed. When I was nine and Janet had been around for two years, we had a turning point, I guess you could call it, over her homework.

"What's wrong?" I said.

"Stupid algebra," she said. "Drives me nuts."

"Let me see."

"What?"

"Let me see," I told her. "I take all these enrichment classes since nobody knows what to do with me. I take advanced math."

"All this time with you," she said, "and I never knew you were a little prodigy. I mean, I knew you were crazy, and you have a big vocabulary for your age, and you're strong, but we never talked about school."

"I keep it secret."

"Uh-huh," she said. "Well, here it is."

I took her homework. "We can do this one of two ways," I said. "I can give you the answers, or you can do it with me to understand."

Janet laughed: "I'll do it with you, handsome."

I nearly choked. At this exact moment, I got confused and thought she might be you. I was confused a long time.

"You would be my wife if we were grown up." That's what I said, two years later.

"I don't know, Erik. You're scary." That's how Janet Gill answered.

I was eleven, and she didn't come as often as she used to. She split her time between high school and ballet. Now she dances for one of the famous companies—ABT, I think—but then she still took outside lessons. I hardly needed the sitting, since I'd gotten tall and strong for my age.

"Maybe you're already my wife," I said. "Husbands and wives help each other survive. They hold each other in their hearts. I've given this a lot of thought, Janet."

Janet laughed. "You can't be my husband, Erik." She laid her head on her arm and stared up at me, dreamy and smiling. "Even though I can't think of anyone better for the job," she said, "we're a lot too young for that kind of talk." Then she kissed me. She lifted her head and kissed my cheek. "I wish the guys I'm around all day had your depth. They don't."

I didn't move a muscle. She'd just broken my heart and taught me a lesson. Everything inside me, everything solid, organs and bones, turned to water. I sloshed and slooshed. I'd made a mistake. You, my true love, would never deny me.

"Who are you?" Janet said. "What are you?" She put her hand on my shoulder. "You're a strange one. A superboy. You'll be a superhero. Everyone will wonder about you. You'll be loved and hated. Your enemies will want to destroy the world and kidnap me. I'll say, I knew him when his muscles were small and he was half my size. I'll tell people, He did my homework for me at nine, and one day I kissed him." She pulled me closer

31

by the shoulder and kissed my cheek again. She kissed my ear. Then she whispered: "Are you ready?"

I nodded.

"I will never babysit for you after this, and we might never see each other again."

"I know," I said.

"Then we both know."

Her lips trembled, and I wondered if she had ever kissed anyone before. When would she have time between high school and rehearsal?

The dry, shaking kiss came. She bit my lip. For a long second, she wouldn't let go.

No magic or miracle other than this. An older girl kissed a younger boy, a boy much older than she'd ever be.

When my mother returned home, she sensed something had changed. Her eyes switched from Janet to me and back again. "Something happen?"

"Mrs. Lynch," she said, "I told Erik first, but I can't come here anymore. I don't think he needs me, and I dance too much. I don't have the time."

"Oh." My mother caught my eye. "I guess I wish you'd spoken to me first, Janet, but it's really Erik you have to care for. I understand your decision. We'll miss you. Erik especially. We'll keep track when you're famous."

"That would be nice, Mrs. Lynch. Thank you." Janet put her hand on my shoulder and turned me toward her. "Give me a hug." For what seemed like a century, I watched her face and her never-ending neck. She held me and whispered into my ear. "Maybe, Erik, maybe one day, real love."

"Well, here," my mother said and handed Janet her last pay. They hugged, and Janet left.

My mother closed the door after her. "Are you sure nothing happened, Erik? That seemed very awkward. I felt like I interrupted you two."

"What could you have interrupted, Mama? She was my minder."

"Well, what did she whisper?"

"Nothing," I said.

"She whispered something, Erik."

"Nothing important. Just good-bye."

"And your lip?"

I touched my mouth.

For the first time, I lied to my mother. I betrayed my mother, and for another little while, a month or more, I kept silent.

Wife

SOMETIME IN THE FUTURE, when I'm older, I will know you, my true love, at first sight. People won't believe me. They'll call me crazy or, worse, stupid. You'll look at me right away as if you own me. You'll look at me with some mixture of love, kindness, gentleness, and whatever else a woman has in her eyes when she looks at her true love. Then we'll decide to take a walk together, and on the walk, you'll say, "I can't believe I found you," and I'll say, "Who am I?"

"My husband," you'll say.

"And who are you?" I'll say.

"Your wife," you'll say.

"There it is," I'll say.

We'll kiss. We'll kiss. I'll pick you up in my arms, right there, on the street and walk with you, kissing you, until we pass by a couple of kids who'll start laughing at us, and then I'll put you down, and we'll hold hands, walk for a time in silence, until I say, "We have to find our home."

I've never wanted a girlfriend. I've never wanted to go on dates. I've only wanted a wife.

That's right. But for now, you are you, only you, all you, un-discovered.

Food

4:32 A.M. I'M SITTING at the dining table with a bowl of Hearty Oats cereal flooded in my mother's half-and-half. I can see her asleep in the armchair, her neck craned. She can't possibly be comfortable, but she sleeps. I eat my cereal. It's good. I like raisin bran more, oatmeal even more, soft-boiled eggs a little more, which come in behind scrambled, and scrambled a mile from over easy, which can't hold a candle to a ham sandwich on wheat with mustard and mayo, itself in the shadow of a salami sandwich on anything, with anything, and the salami may only wish it were sardines, the sardines wanting to be liverwurst and onions on rye with spicy mustard, and the liverwurst dying of longing to be a bowl of chocolate pudding, the chocolate pudding ecstatic to be anything like my mother's meat loaf, but even my mother's meat loaf would trade its onions to be a slab of poached salmon, a tuna sandwich, or pickled herring in wine, which finds itself narrowly beaten by mussels or clams. If I'm not a seal, I'm an otter.

I do like a skinny piece of skirt steak with pepper, mashed sweet potatoes, and baby peas. I like English muffins with butter. Peanut butter, but leave off the jelly. Bananas have to be green, plums hard, and peaches soft. I can eat my weight in blueberries. Strawberries are gold. Anchovy pizza, yes. Vinegar, yes. Lettuces, yes. Spinach and kale, no. Arugula, yes, since it's peppery. I don't like candy, but I like chocolate chip cookies. Ice cream, chocolate ice cream, oh yes, and chocolate malts make me very happy. Pumpkin pie, though, is my favorite dessert. I like to drink milk almost exclusively. Why drink anything else? Seriously, with the exception of apple juice, can you think of a reason to drink anything else?

Alone

NOTHING RUINS SILENCE QUICKER than the voice of another person. I hear a voice, and I have to listen, even for a second, if only to decide whether or not it's worth listening to. Why? We're hardwired to listen for each other's call.

For the first time in I don't know how long, I walked with Nick, Holly, Jerome, and Martin after school. I don't know how it happened, but somehow I ended up walking with them, or they ended up walking with me.

"Erik." Jerome, the athlete, punched me in the shoulder, and my whole arm went numb. I almost cried out, almost hit him, almost cursed, but I held it all back and started laughing.

"Wait," Holly said, "get him a piece of paper and pen so he can write *ouch*."

Martin laughed. "Or, *You son of a bitch, I'm going to kill you.*"

Nick slid his arm around my shoulder. "Erik, my brother, what's going on?"

"Interpretive dance?" Holly again.

All of us laughed, and Jerome said, "At least he's a good sport."

Then tall Martin put his hand on my head. My head like an acorn in the hand of a grizzly. "How can you say no?" he said.

"Come sit with us," Nick said. "We're going for French fries and shakes. You can sit there smiling like a chimp, not a word, if you want."

The five of us, the quintuplet, a word I love, though I like quincunx more, stood in the middle of the sidewalk, the four of them looking at me, and me looking back at the four of them.

"Please, Erik," Holly said. "This once, and we'll leave you alone."

I should have said yes. I should have gone. Maybe if I had, I would've gotten them back. Other than you, who will I have when the story of my life comes to an end?

Mercy

I WALKED BY MY mother this morning on my way to the kitchen. She was asleep in her armchair. It was later than she ever sleeps. I poured her a glass of orange juice, and I brought it to her.

I tapped her shoulder. Nothing. I never touch her while she sleeps, since I never want to wake her up. But I touched her again, and she jerked awake.

"What?" she said. "Everything okay?" Her eyes were wild and unfocused. "Erik, are you all right?"

I nodded and pointed to the clock. Almost seven thirty.

"I'm sick," she said. She took the juice and drank a little. "Thank you, sweetheart. I have to call in."

I got the phone from the sofa table.

"No, no," she said. "I'll use the one in my bedroom."

I noticed immediately, but it wasn't until my mother got to the door of the bedroom, holding her blanket around herself, clutching it under her chin, that she looked back at me and heard herself again in her own ear.

My bedroom, she'd said. My bedroom.

Overnight, she lost something of my father, the tightness of his grip loosened up, and she was saved.

Do you think my touch made a difference? If I had put my hand on her years ago, while she dreamed of my father, or between her dreams, would she have healed sooner? Did I close up the hole in my mother's heart?

Question

HOW LONG SHOULD A miracle last?

I hear people talk about the miracle of nature, and I know what they mean. Nature has always been and always will be, as far as my tiny brain can understand, miraculous. Except, nature won't last because the world won't. It's a known fact our sun will explode. When our sun explodes, it will take away from the universe everything I have ever known or could imagine, and everything behind and ahead of me. I don't know how this figures in with God.

A miracle will last as long as a god or God allows it. A minute or an hour or centuries. A miracle might last as long as there's a world and nature where it can live. Or it will end when the world ends.

Maybe, though, maybe you and I will be a supermiracle. How can we know we won't go past the end of the world, past time, even past God?

Who says we won't?

Red

I'M BLEEDING. I JUST noticed. It's slow. An oozing, not even a trickle. From a hundred little holes in my forehead. The blood won't stop.

What would you say about this? What could you say?

How did this happen? It's like finding a bruise on your arm and having no idea how it got there. I have nowhere to go for answers.

A miracle, right? A fresh miracle.

I'm used to my unknowing. I don't even know when to be afraid. I mean, is there anything more frightening about blood than an immortal flower or a water stain or my mother's healing?

Easter week.

Concern

MY HEAD STARTED BLEEDING first. Now blood seeps from holes in my wrists. And just like that, a slow bleeding to death.

I wear a hat, long sleeves, and fingerless gloves, even inside, like it's some kind of phase. How long can I get away with it? Spring has sprung.

The End of the Beginning

EASTER SUNDAY, AND WHILE some kids hunt for eggs, I bleed.

My blood smells dark. Like what? Like a pine.

Evergreen sap.

Invisible thorns prick my head so the blood drips down through my lashes and into my eyes. The blood glues and tangles up my hair.

My punctured wrists weep blood. I bleed from holes in my feet.

All this blood makes me think I'll die young.

This morning, when I woke up, my pillow was sticky with blood. I decided I had to talk with my mother. I wanted her to wrap my hands in bandages, to wrap my feet and my head.

I had to break my silence. The sound of my voice made her cry, but I had to get her to listen.

"Erik," she said, "you're scaring me. What are you talking about?"

"Close your eyes," I said.

"Oh, Erik," she protested, but she closed her eyes. "Really, you're scaring me. I just want to hear your voice."

"Please," I said. "Wait."

I took off my hat and gloves, my socks, my long-sleeve T-shirt.

"Okay," I said. "You can look."

My mother opened her eyes. For a moment, she said nothing, and I knew she must have felt shocked into silence.

I held out my hands, and she took them in hers.

Another moment, and then she said, "What am I supposed to be looking for, honey?"

"What do you mean?" I said.

"You have me confused."

"Don't you see the blood? It's all over me."

My mother turned my hands over, then back again. She shook her head.

I was suddenly afraid. The wounds were bleeding. Why couldn't my mother see this?

"Erik?"

"Hm?" I took my hands back. I laughed. "Nothing. I'm awake."

"Is it a headache?"

"No, I'm fine. Nightmare. I thought I was bleeding. I'm sorry."

"You scared me, you know?" She kissed my forehead. I saw my blood smeared on her lips. "Let me get you breakfast. We'll talk all morning."

My invisible wounds. I have no answer, no proof I bleed. But I bleed. Sure as I love my mother and you, I bleed.

THORN

VOICES IN MY HEAD. Growls and grunts and whining saws.

◇

A woman got on the train and pushed right past me. She sat on the floor. Tote bags between her legs. The crush of people, so I turned a little to see her. No one wanted to stand too close. She had sunglasses on, huge ones that fit over regular glasses. She looked old, but I wasn't sure. She didn't have any teeth. And her hair was dyed an unnatural shade of red or something closer to orange. I thought I saw gray underneath. I don't know. She might have been old and suffered a lot. Or she might have been young and suffered her whole life.

She talked to herself. Her hands flew around like frightened birds. Something moved inside of her. Spirits.

Homeless? Who knows?

There she was, on the terrible floor. High socks held up with rubber bands, and her skirt falling down her legs. She didn't care, and I didn't look away. I don't know why. What does a crazy woman wear under her skirt?

Then I noticed something. Her legs. Her legs were young. I expected wrinkles or spots or veins. And her smooth hands, long elf fingers, knuckles like little skulls.

She was skinny, skinny. When did she last eat? Days or weeks or years? But she had perfect legs and perfect hands.

The train slowed down.

The woman dumped an ancient brown coat and a gold scarf out of a bag right onto the floor. She wrapped the scarf around her head and tied it at the back of her neck. She pushed herself up to her feet, pulled on her coat, lost her balance. She grabbed my shoulder. Her eyes. Black and pink in her sunglasses. Her eyes, or not her eyes exactly, her gaze was a needle. A needle pushed straight through to the back of my skull.

"Get it out of my head," she said. "You look like a nice boy. Get it all out of my head."

I touched her. I held her up. "It'll be better now," I said. What else could I say?

The train stopped. She picked up her bags, slid out, and disappeared into the crowd.

◇

It all might have been a dream. Or did it happen? I can't always tell the difference.

Dreams, memories, what does it matter?

I have a memory from when I was very young. How long out of my mother?

I remember a man lifting me over his head one-handed, two suns shining out of his dark glasses. His mouth filled up with a golden light. This must have been my father.

I remember crawling into an oven and sitting under the coils.

I remember a dark alley and the black points of buildings stabbing the sky.

And I remember a windy day. I was walking next to my mother down on the avenue. The wind lifted me off my feet and sent me flying. My mother couldn't hold on. She screamed. A Doberman pinscher snatched me out of the air and saved me. It dropped me at my mother's feet.

◇

Is even one of these memories true? Or did I make them all up?

They feel true to me.

◇

My hand might be broken. I punched my bureau. I don't know why. I have no idea why.

The power of my heart.

◇

I don't always know who speaks for me or out of me. I am many. I have a Protector who shields me against the world, against people, men, women, and other kids, and against monsters, beasts, and the wild. He's huge and can't be stopped, but he won't protect me against the Sawmen. The

Sawmen punish me if I don't listen to the Architect. When the Sawmen come, I suffer. The severing.

The Guardians command the Sawmen. Geniuses with whips. They will talk with me, but when they talk, they growl. They laugh when there's nothing funny at all. They laugh at me because I'm stupid compared to them, compared to the Architect. They serve the Architect with total loyalty.

The Architect lives at the center of me. He created everything within me, and I sometimes think he created me, too. I've never seen him, and I can't imagine him. I know he thinks and draws and stares out of the windows of my eyes.

Who created the Architect? What was inside me before him? Anything?

◇

A drop of rain hits the window and dissolves. Another one and another one.

Thunder, lightning.

Rain scared me when I was young. Not even so long ago. Splash splash splash splash

I will not be killed. Panic. The lightning, the thunder, the rain. Soaked. Keep running. What have I done to die like this?

The frog. The frog.

Sixth grade. Three years ago. My winged mother came out of hell to frighten me. All her screeching and bloody fingers. And my father arrived in fire and pushed my face into my cereal. Nearly drowned me in a bowl of milk. I squirmed out and ran the five flights from our apartment to the ground floor. Escaped.

My face. Milk running down my face under my shirt, dripping all over my shirt. Milk in my ears. Milk coming out my nose. Milk streaming from my eyes.

Out in the street, I pulled my baseball cap down low. I had my backpack, my apartment key in my left front pocket, and stuff in my right front pocket. A stone, a bottle cap, a tiny key to a hidden lock, and some change. My sneakers looked new, but the treads had been worn down. I went through a pair of sneakers every month before I stopped growing. All my running and walking.

My pants above my ankles—high-waters. Always embarrassed and ugly. I still have the ankles of a pony, too skinny for my legs.

My backpack. Pencils and erasers. Binder. A separate math notebook. A worn copy of *Bridge to Terabithia* I had to read for class, and a few other tools of the trade. A silver cross on a chain I kept all by itself in a pocket. Lunch in a brown paper bag, a sandwich and cookies that I'd give up or throw out. I had these books: *The Pilgrim's Progress* and *One Flew Over the Cuckoo's Nest. Catcher in the Rye,* which

I thought would have a bad ending and did. Totally boring and meaningless. Very human.

The school day started like any other. A settling of home-work with Mrs. Jacobs. New stuff, whatever it might've been. Who cares?

Then, Kristine Pierre passed me a note. She had to know what would happen. She sprang the trap. The note came through Kristine, who tucked it into my collar since she sat behind me.

Meet me after school on the back steps. Just you. Mala.

The rest of the day was a waste. I went around in a fog. I couldn't keep my eyes off Mala for months. She came here from Bangladesh. I'm not even sure if Mala's her real name. She might have a Bengali name too hard for me to pronounce. She has black hair almost too thick to believe, a real ponytail. Her eyes are the size of dinner plates and only seem black. I once saw the sun in her eye. Deep brown.

She smiles like a voice inside of her tells her she's beau-tiful and loved. Only a half smile, but happy. Her skin is dark. Dark and light at the same time.

She made me stupid.

The day went by until it ended. I stuffed my backpack and sat in the corner of the classroom after the last bell. Waiting, terrified. Calm down. Calm down. I had to get myself together.

I got to the back stairs and the locked door the janitors use. No Mala, so I waited.

Five minutes, ten minutes, a year.

Finally. Mala. Mala, covered in sun.

I smiled. Stupid, stupid. I smiled.

Mala. Then, after Mala, after the dream, I woke up.

What was this? Another girl, another girl, three boys, two more girls, one girl and two boys, until half of the sixth grade, some part of the fifth grade, maybe a fourth grader or two stood in front of me. It's hard to count when you think you're going to explode in fear and shame. The laughing started. I couldn't make out who was standing there laughing.

The laughing mob, a bright white devil walking on split hooves, came closer. I wanted to escape. I took the steps too fast. I tripped and fell face-first in front of the devil. She picked up her shining goat heel and crushed my left hand. The tip of my left ring finger. The nail would fall off a week later. At that moment, I yelped and snarled. I was a kicked dog. I got to my feet, pushed my way through the crowd.

The last person was Mala, behind the beast. At the back of the crowd. It made no sense. She looked sad. No sense.

Her hair almost caught my ankle. I would've fallen down again.

I ran and ran. Opposite from home, so I had farther to walk

once I stopped. On one block or another, something caught my eye, a frog in the street. Tears, rage, shame, pain, and still I see a frog trying to make its way across the street. I stood on the sidewalk, watching the frog. I looked up and down the street. No traffic. How long could this last?

Come on, frog. Jump. Thinking. Thinking. *Jump, frog. Get out of the street.*

Why didn't I walk out into the street and grab the frog, save it, drop it into someone's front yard?

Jump, frog.

The frog jumped and jumped, but it was still in the street. My anger. *What are you doing? Jump. You're almost here.*

Cars drove past in both directions. One missed the frog by a hair.

Come on. Jump.

The frog. Stupid, so stupid. What kind of creature lets itself get caught in the middle of the street? I walked into the road and picked up the frog. My stomped finger throbbed, and I started crying. I crunched my teeth. I swore revenge.

Revenge on who? Mala? The goat?

I crushed the frog.

The frog survived the street, the traffic, and I killed it. It died in my hand.

I'm sorry.

I threw its body into a hedge and wiped my hand on my jeans. "I'm sorry." I said it out loud. "I'm sorry. I'm sorry. I'm sorry."

Then the rain came.

Splash splash splash splash

Lightning.

I should be killed for killing the frog. I don't want to die. I run.

I call for help. Please let me live, dear God. Please let me live.

Thunder everywhere and the unbelievable rain and the lightning and the breaking frog and my splashing.

◇

The frog. Thinking about it right now, all kinds of time and other terrible things happening since then. I still get sick about that frog. But would I do it again? I don't know, which is almost as bad as saying yes.

◇

A lot of blood. A nail through my foot. A bone, my ulna, snapped in two and breaking the skin. Blood vessels in my eyes. My wrists, my hands, and skull. Lips and knees. My brain, my stomach. Ears.

Scars. Yes.

How? Cigarettes, an iron, hammer, nail, fist, fingers. Belt. Cysts. Chicken pox. Stairs. Slippery grass and a rock. Popped bicycle tire. Tine test. Acne.

Why? I don't always know. Some of this was my fault. Being foolish. Most of it not. Most of it done to me by my father and mother.

Did I mention razors? Train tracks?

◇

Crying against a wall. Disintegrating. Sobbing. In public, a public mall. Corner. Nothing behind. Nothing now. Nothing ahead.

◇

I always get fevers whenever I'm sick, high fevers, dangerous fevers. The kind that cook the brain like an egg in its shell. Hard to know if these fevers are really my body fighting infection or if they're the battles between my minds that come so close to the surface.

This time, I woke up with a tattoo on my right forearm. The letter *F*. In black, just below the scar where my ulna broke the skin, and the letter was bleeding. Blood smeared down to my hand. Fingerprints. Not just the tips, whole fingers, someone holding my arm. Maybe the person who gave me the tattoo. One of my Guardians? Or my mother? I don't know. What does *F* signify? Fire? Frenzy? Fever? Fuel? Fall?

The letter bleeds, and it won't stop. Or am I bleeding at all? I can't tell.

◇

On the other side of my bedroom wall, there's another apartment. In that apartment, there's a man. This man owns guns. If I press my ear to the wall, I can hear him pulling triggers and making the sounds of little explosions with his mouth.

Pow, pow, pow.

◇

A trestle where I thought I'd die. I had to do a lot to get there. I had to fight through the Sawmen and the Guardians. The saws.

I sat on the bridge, looking down at the tracks. The wood, stones, and rails. How long before a freight train comes through?

Then, as I sat there, prepared and ready, another me showed up. He stood on the bridge, a witness. He didn't judge me. He didn't beg me to jump or beg me to think again. He had no emotion at all. He was me, a little older, a little taller.

Then, another me, a third Thorn, appeared. He stood behind the second me. Definitely wider and taller; he could see over the second Thorn's head. Not a man, not yet, and he, too, didn't say a word.

I stood up and walked over to them. I looked back on the me sitting with his legs over the side of the bridge, waiting to jump. The fall would've broken my legs in front of an approaching train. No escape.

I started thinking.

You've been shortsighted. You haven't seen anything, done anything.

I thought and thought.

You haven't climbed a mountain. You've never gone anywhere on your own. What do you know about anything?

I watched myself for a little while longer.

You've never been in love.

I slid off the bridge onto the sidewalk. The other Thorns, already gone, had disappeared into me or the air.

◇

The Sawmen made me suffer. I felt their blades. I bled from my stomach, my spine split, and they cut me in half again and again. The Architect's punishment for my thoughts of suicide.

I survived myself. Doesn't this mean I'll survive everything and everyone?

◇

I was halfway across a street, but the woman in the car didn't want to stop for the sign. She wanted to slide by. At the last second, she realized she couldn't make the turn without hitting me. She stopped short. I glared at her and brought my fist down on the hood of her car. "What the hell are you doing?"

What did she do? She raised her hands and shouted back

through her windshield. I could read her lips: "What? I stopped."

I argued with myself whether or not to hit her car again.

Things happen inside of me, and sometimes they come out. I brought my hand down, laid my palm on the hood, and the engine stopped. The tires deflated, all four of them, flat to their rims, and I glued the woman's hands to the steering wheel. I willed her window down. She couldn't speak.

"You've got to watch the people," I said. My voice sounded deep and foreign, even to me: my Protector. "You've got to watch the people."

Minutes went by before my mind and heart were mine again. Then the sadness came.

I released the woman's hands, started the car, inflated the tires, and gave her back her tongue. An angry miracle.

◇

My name is Hawthorn Blythe. I had a sister named Salome. Her name comes from the Hebrew word for peace. *Shalom.* She drowned when I was four. Saving my life. All I remember is the taste of the ocean. Salome turned into a seahorse. I'd swear it.

Her bedroom looks exactly like it did when she was thirteen. A few posters on the wall, certificates of merit in swimming and medals, but, mostly, there's the sheet music. Sheet music on her walls, books of sheet music piled on her bed, just as she left them, the top one open to Corelli's Allegro in D Major, no. 11, from *Twenty-Four Preludes*. She played piano, violin, and guitar. She sang. I have nothing on her. I can't sing or play a thing. Nothing on her, except for chess. How can chess compare to music? It can't.

Salome loved me. This must be obvious. Before she died, my parents loved me, too.

My parents were named Kermit and Tatiana. Once they fell into their Gehenna, as my father called it, they lost their names. Nameless demons. They visit me from hell. The violence against me started ten years ago.

◇

Punishment.

◇

My parents stopped feeding me and themselves more or less. They gave me bologna or peanut butter, water or tea. I have no idea what they ate. I never saw them sit down to dinner. Where did they eat? What kept them alive? Their anger? Their hate? Their violence?

◇

My nameless parents. I want to give them new names. Kulthat for my father and, for my mother, Tillion. Kulthat and Tillion, the demons who slowly kill me.

Hawthorn Blythe.

Hawthorn. My father told me the same information over and over before he became a demon. "Thorn, your namesake comes from a fruit-bearing shrub and tree. Family: Rosaceae. Genus: Crataegus. The plant has much myth and lore around it, from faeries to druids to Christ Himself. I have favorites. Hawthorn kills vampires dead, so to speak. It may heal a broken heart. Christ's crown of thorns came from a hawthorn, and so it groans and cries out on Good Friday."

I have never killed a vampire. I've only broken hearts. I believe I could torture Christ.

Blythe=*blithe*. According to the dictionary, *blithe* means "joyous, merry, or gay in disposition; cheerful." Or "without thought or regard; heedless; carefree." Do I have to say anything?

Hawthorn Blythe. Is this any kind of name for an unhappy killer who thinks too much?

◇

Chess. Kermit taught me when I was very young, before Salome died.

My father had been a prodigy, though he lost interest. He went to law school at nineteen. Now he does nothing, has nothing.

Could I be called a prodigy? Hard to say. I've never played chess against anyone but my father.

The day Salome died, my father and I played a game. On the beach, in the sand, a travel set. I took a floating raft out on the ocean. My father had me in check, and I needed to think. Could I save myself from mate?

I put my head down. When I looked up, ready to come in with my escape, I'd drifted so far out. What could I do? I screamed.

My sister stood on the beach scanning for me. Her hand shading her eyes. When she heard me, she came to me. A rescue that would leave her dead.

◇

I don't exactly play chess anymore. I have no one to play against. I work out the puzzles in the newspaper. I play against myself.

Is chess a violent game? It's war on a board. So it's violent at its source.

I've played more than once against Kulthat, my father who's not my father. Now a demon. When one of us takes a piece, we make the other bleed. A dagger here, a sword there, an ax, a mace, an arrow. We suffer. We finish games fainting.

I always win. How could I not? Kulthat forgets he needs to plan. It's a war, and wars need plans. It needs more than just the desire to damage your opponent, to punish him for breaking your heart. For killing your daughter.

◇

I feel safe when I take a shower. I don't know why, but the Sawmen, the Guardians, the Protector, the minds, everybody, they all go quiet. My half memories disappear. I stand in the hot water, and I lean against the wall. The tiles are cool. I stand for a long time, sometimes until the heat runs out of the water. I slump against the wall and almost fall asleep standing up. Occasionally, I feel like crying. I wonder if I'll cry harder than I've ever cried. Then nothing comes.

Sometimes, like this morning, I feel like I'm going to throw up. That passes.

◇

My fifth-grade teacher hit me.

I drove him to it.

"Thorn, for the last time, I know you stole the money. I know it, John knows it, the class knows it. Simple as that." Mr. Holt loosened his tie. The blue tie with a yellow fish, dreaming of itself with legs. "Thorn, are you listening?"

I slouched in my chair and picked at a scab of glue in the palm of my hand. I looked at him: "What?"

"What are you listening to, Thorn, if you're not listening to me?" Holt crossed his arms. "Why am I talking to you when I could be on my way home? It's Friday. It's three fifteen. Why am I here?"

I sighed.

This made Holt furious. What was it? My rudeness and carelessness and boredom? That's what he said. He wanted to slap me. I could tell. I've seen the look a thousand times. Kulthat. Kulthat hit me and hit me and hit me. I remember the narrow fire-eyes.

Holt clenched his teeth and combed his hair with his fingers. Then he smiled. A smile without the smile. "Look," he said. "I'm sorry, Thorn. I got carried away."

Silence.

"Thorn," Holt said, soft as soft can be. "Where's John's money?"

"I don't know. Really, Mr. Holt, I don't know."

Holt squatted in front of me. He put down his fists like two stones on my desk. "Thorn?"

"I didn't take it," I said.

What could Holt do? He had no solid proof either way, so he dismissed me. He asked me to close the door.

I watched him through the window.

Mr. Holt sat at his desk with his head in hands. He must've wondered what in the end kept him from hitting me. I'm sure of it. I could hear him thinking: *He can't be allowed to get away with it. One good, hard smack—*.

The very next Monday, Holt described an incident between a boy and a barber to my homeroom. "This boy, Jimmy, needed a haircut. The boy, about your age, walked by a barbershop.

He asked the barber how much for a haircut, and the barber told him to get lost."

The class couldn't believe it. "He didn't tell the kid?"

"No," Holt said.

"That's just wrong," the class said. "What'd the kid do?"

"What could he do?" Holt said. "He walked away."

"He walked away?" At this point, the class blew apart into a dozen small discussions.

Holt watched us. I watched Holt.

"Enough," Holt said. He went to his desk. "We have other things to do."

My class discussed strategies for dealing with a barber. A rude barber. Holt went through his handouts.

"Mr. Holt?"

Holt answered without looking up: "Yes?"

"That happened to you, didn't it?"

Silence.

"Who said that?"

"You went to the barber," I said. "Not some kid. Right?"

"No, Thorn." Holt tried not to explode. He kept on pretending to look over his papers. "Though every one of us has a story like that."

"A story like what, Mr. Holt?" Not me this time. Candace Ingram. All curls and teeth.

"Like the one I just told." Holt turned red. "Sometimes strangers are rude to us."

"Oh," Candace said. "The way the barber was rude to you?"

"No," Holt said, but we all knew. His tone of voice and his redness. His eyes swirling like soup. "Now, let's get back to work. And Thorn? See me at the end of the day."

"Thorn, we've had our run-ins." Holt leaned back in his chair, crossed his legs, and locked his fingers on top of his head. "But I thought we came away from those times as friends. I was prepared to forget last Friday because we're friends. Right, Thorn?"

I peeled a Band-Aid off my thumb. With my teeth.

"Right?" Holt looked at the ceiling. "Thorn?"

"What?"

"Why do you do that?" Holt's anger spilled out again. "We're friends, yes?" he said.

I shrugged. "I guess." I opened the cut on my thumb, and it bled.

Holt watched as I stopped the bleeding with my T-shirt.

"Thorn?" Holt bent forward in his chair. "Do you remember the story I told this morning?"

"Yes."

"What would you have done with the barber?"

I checked my thumb. "I wouldn't've walked away."

Holt cleared his throat. "Yes, that's probably true. But what would you have done?"

"Was it you?" I spoke to my bleeding thumb. "I won't tell. I just want to know."

Holt loosened his green knit tie and unbuttoned his collar. "Did you steal that money from John?"

"Yes," I lied. Strong. Who knows what happened to the dum-dum's money? "I stole it."

"You—"

I interrupted him. "So was it you in the story?"

"I swear I'll have you thrown out of this school."

"Whatever," I said. "You can't stand up to a man, and you can't stand up to a boy."

Holt pushed his chair away and walked to the classroom door. He shook as he closed the door.

I knew what was coming. I wanted him to do it.

"It was you. Just say it. It doesn't matter. A rude and stupid barber: so what? Like you said, we all have stories. Just say it."

"Shut up, Thorn, shut up."

"Just say it, Mr. Holt." I stood up. "Just say, 'The barber was rude to me, and I couldn't do anything about it.' Say it."

"Thorn."

"Say it, Mr. Holt. I know it's you. Tell the truth. Say it's you. Say it. Say it, and we can go home."

The slap, when it came, crumpled me against the desk. I must have cried out. But Holt would've heard only a hum coming from his right hand. A hum surrounded by silence.

We are the Guardians. We speak. Listen to us.

Human beings.

Human beings. All of you. We know your kind.

nocourage notruth nocourage notruth nocourage notruth nocourage notruth nocourage notruth nocourage notruth nocourage notruth

no courage no truth

We know your kind. You don't want to think, you don't want to care, you don't want to have mercy, you don't want to show consideration. You want your comfort. You want your protection.

No truth. No courage.

Worthless.

◇

A pigeon followed me. "Go away." The bird kept coming. "Get away from me." It went up the front steps of the apartment building, and as I went up in the elevator, I heard it walking up the façade, up the concrete walls, up and up, its talons clicking. Why didn't it fly?

The pigeon found my room. It started pecking a hole through the glass of my window. It stopped only to tell me one thing. "It's no use," it said. "I'll get to you." I heard it as if it were on the inside of the glass, not on the outside.

How could a pigeon talk to me? And how could it kill me? Did Kulthat send it out of hell?

"This is ridiculous," I said. "You can't kill me."

"Watch me."

"I'll kill you first." This seemed like a good idea. "I'll kill you first. I'll kill you first."

"No you won't."

I opened the window, and the pigeon swelled up. I grabbed it, and it pecked at my fingers. My knuckles. I got angry.

I crushed it in my hands. Once I saw a bus run over a pigeon, and the bird burst like a paper bag filled with air. POP!

Those hollow bones broke. POP!

This happened with the demon-bird. It popped. Then it disappeared from my hands. I stood at the window. Blood on my face, my shirt, my hands. The pigeon gone, gone like it was never there.

◇

The pigeon had disappeared. I couldn't speak, but I felt something on my tongue. A word?

It grew out of my tongue like a flower, or a blade of grass. It tickled the roof of my mouth. I couldn't bear it. When I opened my mouth, a feather, gray, an inch long, swirled out. The feather rocked back and forth, back and forth, and landed in my hand. I shut my mouth.

What was I to think?

I tried to keep my mouth shut, I tried, but my cheeks swelled with feathers. They tickled my throat, the roof of my mouth. My teeth. I blew out a mouthful, and they scattered over my head. The wind caught them. They collided, rose up, and fell.

More and more feathers. They swirled and tumbled. Feathers streamed from my mouth until they stopped.

This happened.

◇

"You are a most unusual young man."

Who said it?

The Architect? A Guardian? My Protector? Who?

"You shouldn't die. You should live. I will help you live."

"Why?" I said it out loud. "Why? What will I do? What's my purpose? I'm nothing."

"No."

"I'm nothing. I'm nothing. I'm nothing. I'm nothing."

I cried.

"I'm nothing. I'm nothing."

◇

Silence.

◇

I wish all the voices I hear inside my head would melt down into one voice, a voice I can trust.

◇

I shave. If I don't shave, I have this little beard and dirty mustache. Tufts of hair come out of my neck and one cheek. It's ridiculous.

I used Kulthat's electric razor one time without asking. He wrapped the cord around my neck and shaved part of my arm.

I once used Tillion's razor. The one she uses for her legs. She screamed at me. "It's useless. I cut open my ankle, you little wretch." She sat me down and shaved my chin and lip and neck and cheek without using any soap and water. Against the grain of my skin.

I burned, and blood ran down my face and throat.

I don't like to think about my childhood. Until I was almost five, Kermit and Tatiana provided for me, loved me. Then everything changed. Salome's death. Poverty. My parents turning into demons that fly from their hell to punish and kill. The starvation and neglect.

I found a razor that took the old-fashioned double-edged blades. In the bathroom cabinet. It had a black handle. Kermit must have used it once. The first time I used it just with water and the old blade. A rusted edge. Mistake. Cracks, scratches, fire, and blood.

Late at night. My face hurting me. Hundreds of little cuts bleeding and burning.

How would I buy new blades and shaving cream? I couldn't ask Tillion and Kulthat. They would have said no to lending me money. I checked my room. I found sixty-three cents on the floor. Four pennies in my sock drawer. Sixty-seven cents. I needed a drink of water.

I crept toward the kitchen opposite Kulthat and Tillion's room. I crept, but Tillion still called, "Thorn?"

"Yes, ma'am. Just need a drink."

Tillion came to the door in her robe. Disheveled from sleep and green light pouring out of her ears. "Come here," she said and reached out her arm. I dreamed my mother, my real mother, would lend me the money to get what I needed. I wouldn't even have to pay her back. Or, better, she would get it all for me.

Not this, but something almost as strange happened. Tillion became Tatiana for a moment. My mother, Tatiana, put her hand on my head. "No fever," she said, and kissed my forehead. She must have been in a dream. Dreaming I'm worth something.

"I just need a drink."

I found Tillion's purse on the kitchen counter. I unsnapped it and waited to see if this tiny sound would bring the demons running from their hell-room. They didn't come.

I took eight dollars, snapped the purse shut, and returned to my room. I forgot to pour some water.

◇

The next morning, I stopped at the drugstore. I asked the employee where I could find razors and shaving cream. "You need it for sure," the guy said.

I got angry. I said, "Nobody asked you."

"Oho, little man. Keep your voice down. Aisle eight."

I spent six dollars or so. I felt miserable. All day, my guilt and worry nauseated me. I left school wishing I could go somewhere other than home. I hoped Tatiana, or Tillion, hadn't missed the money.

Tillion, snow and fire and light, had missed it. She waited for me at the front gate.

Silence. Tillion and I walked five minutes without a word. Finally, she spoke.

"Eight dollars has real value to me. Eight dollars is food. Eight dollars goes to our rent."

I said nothing.

"So what did you do with the money, Thorn? What could you possibly have needed it for? And why did you need it so desperately you had to steal it from me?"

"I didn't," I said.

Tillion gripped my arm in her talon. She stopped me in the street. "You didn't take eight dollars from my purse?"

71

"No, ma'am," I said. "I didn't."

"A thief and a liar, is that it? A coward?" My mother buried her nails in my arm. "Open your bag."

"What?"

"You say, 'Pardon, ma'am?' You heard me, mister." Tillion reached for my backpack. "Open it. Dump everything out."

I did as told and turned over my bag onto the sidewalk.

"What did you buy? What did you buy?" Tillion searched all the pockets. Mumbling. She found nothing, no trace of her money, and she hesitated.

At this moment of hesitation, I knew I was safe. I guessed she'd already started to ask herself where she lost her money. How she could be so careless.

"I didn't take your money."

Tillion, now Tatiana all over again, my mother, packed up my bag. "I'm sorry, Thorn, I thought—." We walked. "But why were you so quiet?"

"I don't feel so good."

The tone in Tatiana's voice, the confusion and regret when she apologized to me cut into my stomach. I felt sick with guilt. Even so, I wouldn't admit my robbery. I wanted her to think the best of me. No thief and liar. She put her wrist against my forehead for the second time in a day. Told me she thought I had a slight fever, and I felt a little better. I imagined staying in bed under her care for the rest of my life. She would bring me toast and ginger ale every so often.

The razor blades and cream? The razor from home? All at school. My locker. I shave when I have to, after school, in the boys' bathroom.

Two days ago, Candace Ingram—still mostly teeth and curls, taller—showed up while I was rinsing. I opened my eyes, and there she was, in the mirror, over my shoulder. I nearly screamed.

"Where did you come from?"

"Ninja moves."

"Ninja?"

"I've been dying to know what you do in here. Now I know."

"And?"

"And nothing. Maybe I can shave the back of your neck sometime."

"—?"

"Your hair gets kind of long on your neck. I sit behind you. I've noticed."

"—?"

"I could do it now," she said. "If you want."

❖

The whole time she stood behind me, sliding that razor over my neck, I thought my backbone would break through my skin. It felt that way. I thought I'd fall down.

73

Everybody in me, my Protector, my Sawmen and Guardians, somewhere, even my Architect, wondered if Candace would cut me open with the razor. Leave me for dead on the floor. I felt their suspicion and rage. I heard their growls. I also felt her fingertips and the razor.

Her face in the mirror. Her lips stretched tight over her teeth. Concentration.

How long will she take? How long? Then—

"Done," she said, and ran the razor under the faucet. "How do you feel?"

I checked my neck for blood. "You were gentle," I said.

"What did you expect?"

"—"

She handed me the razor: "I like you, Thorn. I always have."

I couldn't say the same about her. Until that moment, it had never occurred to me to like anyone especially.

"Don't trust her," the Guardians growled. "Your heart. We will make you suffer if you—."

"We could do this again," she said.

"When?" I said, and the Sawmen found their saws.

"The rate you grow hair," she said, "I'd say tomorrow." And she turned to the door.

"I'm not so sure you're funny," I said.

For once, if someone had asked me what I was feeling, I would have said happy. Even then, as the saws sank in.

◇

What about the change in Tillion? Does she want to transform back into Tatiana? After ten years, why now? I can't figure it out. Kulthat seems only to be Kulthat. Is my mother trying to get out of hell? Why?

I don't know what to do. Every time I try to think about it, I go to sleep. It's as if a Protector flips a switch inside of me, and all I can do is put my head down. Sleep.

◇

> *facilis descensus Averno;*
> *noctes atque dies patet atri ianua Ditis;*
> *sed revocare gradum superasque evadere ad auras,*
> *hoc opus, hic labor est.*

Easy is the descent to Avernus, for the door to the underworld lies open both day and night. To retrace your steps and return to the breezes above, that's the task, that's the toil.

◇

Kulthat quotes this from the *Aeneid*. Avernus is another Gehenna, another hell. Maybe he wants to leave hell, but he's too weak. He won't stop the punishment. He punishes me, but he punishes himself, too.

That day on the beach, he let my sister swim out to me. A thirteen-year-old girl rescuing her almost-five-year-old

75

brother. My father couldn't be bothered to look up from the chessboard. My mother slept.

Why didn't he come out to me? Why did he let his daughter die? Why did we lose our shining star to a game of chess?

◇

My favorite word from chess. *Zugzwang.*

When you have to make a move, but you wish the other player had to move. You want to pass, or miss a turn. You have to move, though. When you do, you're suddenly weak.

Zugzwang.

◇

The man next door must have gotten a new gun.

Pop.

I didn't have to listen so hard to hear him.

Poppoppop.

And you're smoke.

◇

I have this fantasy. My mother will come out of hell. My father, if he can't come out, will die in his Gehenna. I want her to forgive me. I never wanted Salome, their shining star, my shining star, to turn into a seahorse. I want to stop feeling like a monster. Murderer. I want to have one voice in my head, mine.

76

I want to feel normal. I want to be normal.

◇

The rattlecan rushes and rushes. All the stones, pebbles, stones, pebbles rolling around and the clattering clatters. The saws turn. Two, four, six, four saws at angles, spinning. The rattlecan teeters and totters. The stones and pebbles, and the saws cut through me. Arms fall down. Legs sprout legs, and my stomach bleeds.

SIXTEEN

There is a wisdom that is woe; but there is a woe
that is madness.

—Herman Melville, *Moby-Dick, or the Whale*

ERIK

Still

TWO YEARS BLEEDING. NO end. No reason.

This is bad enough, but there's worse.

I haven't found you.

My bleeding's invisible to everyone but myself. You would see, wouldn't you? Only you, and you would take a little time out of your day to clean me up.

You'll have your gauze and your ointment: "I'll just have to do this again later."

"I know."

You wipe up the counter.

"It will stop, Erik, someday."

"Before I die?"

"You're bleeding for a reason." You scrub your hands and take a long time cleaning my blood from your fingernail.

Faces

I SEE FACES ALL over the place. In dust on windowpanes, in carpets, plaster, and the branches of trees, in the folds of clothes thrown onto the back of a chair. A man's death mask—open mouth, bullet hole in his forehead—shows up in the layers of a stone I keep in my pocket. I have a frowning man in a fingerprint.

Once I saw your face in my breath. It was a February night under a streetlight. I can't count how many times since then I've looked for you in the mist.

I spent a lot of time this morning making faces in the bathroom mirror. I was supposed to be showering, but I'd just read about *grimaciers* in one of my father's books. *Grimaciers* were French performers who put on performances of facial expressions in the eighteenth century. I stood in front of the mirror and twisted my face and closed one eye. I used my fingers to stretch my mouth and stick out my tongue, and I opened my eyes as wide as they could go. I pinched my eyes and pulled my hair. I pushed my nose flat, I plugged my nostrils, and I let my mouth do what it wanted. I did this so long I started turning into animals. The animals didn't exist in real life. My skin turned colors. I got hairy, furry, and patterns came up. More than once, my teeth became fangs. A few times, I had a trunk and horns. My eyes turned colors, and I barked and laughed.

I'll tell you what made me stop. I made a face that reminded me of my father, but my face was not really mine or his, and I thought, *That's what he looked like when he died, when the bumper of a car crushed his head.* Purple and his eyes backward, showing white, and his tongue rolling three feet out of his mouth.

New Year

1. Keep up the Latin
2. Read the Four Gospels
3. Write, read, think
4. Row
5. Discover my purpose

I'm always resolved to find you. We won't find each other until we find each other, but I keep an eye open. I search all the time.

Fantasy

THE BATHTUB FILLS UP, and you stand at the window. A snowstorm clobbers the world.

An icicle hangs from the roof. It's thicker than your fist at the top and as long as your arm. The winter tooth scares you. If it broke off and struck a person, it would go through bone. You look from the point of the icicle to the ground twenty feet below. A person would have to be standing in the hedge for the icicle to hit. You test the water with your fingers and turn off the faucet. You settle up to your neck and watch the clouds pass.

In this bathroom, you hold the sponge to your nose and smell my mother's brand of black soap, which was my father's. How long can you think about a sponge? How many times can you squeeze a wet sponge and watch the spill wind around your wrist, forearm, elbow, and biceps?

Headache

THE PAIN IN MY head. The skinny knife, and the hammer and nails. The lights of an enormous city pressed into my left eye, and the green aurora borealis rolling past.

Pain has no language other than growls or grunts. A headache for four days.

Nature

ALL THE MIRACLES OF nature I miss. All the miracles I catch.

My mother cracked an egg this morning and cried out. The egg had the beginning of a chick in it.

An ancient fruit tree of some kind, an apple or cherry, grows in the park a little way from here. Every March, it blooms. Ten thousand pink and white flowers bloom and shake for a week. Then, all the flowers fall, and for a while the tree stands in its own memories. Last week, I went to look at the tree in bloom. I stood under it while the blossoms fell all around. I couldn't begin to understand what held me in place, or if it would ever let me go. I know you're like this tree. What will happen to me when I hear your voice?

Apartment

I'LL TELL YOU SOMETHING that's true. When you come into this apartment, you can stand in any room, reach out your arm, and put your hand on a book or magazine. It might not always be in English. It might be in Spanish, French, Portuguese, Irish, Chinese, or Russian. We have something in Dutch and something in Albanian, and something in a language I can't even guess at. Basque, maybe, or Elvish. This shouldn't matter to me, or to anyone, since it's still text. If I look close enough at the symbols, I can make out a story, a poem, or a true fact. Almost all the books are in English.

You'd be amazed. Right now, in a rack behind the bathroom door, there's a book of political cartoons; a biblical concordance; the *New Yorker Book of Dog Cartoons*; *Getting Even*, by Woody Allen; and a book of math puzzles. There are stacks of books everywhere, and the shelves where books live are all bowed. They'll collapse at some point.

Maeterlinck, *The Treasure of the Humble*, 1899; Westcott, Cynthia, *The Gardener's Bug Book*; Kurlansky, Mark, *Cod*; Voltaire, *Candide*; Williams, Margery, *The Velveteen Rabbit*; Neely, Henry M., *A Primer for Star-Gazers*; *The Collected Works of W. B. Yeats*, Volume 1; Phillips, Mark, and Jon Chappell, *Guitar for Dummies*, 2nd edition; White, Carolyn, *A History of Irish Fairies*; Goldman, William, *The Princess Bride*; Elder, George R., *The Body: An Encyclopedia of Archetypal Symbolism*, Volume

2; Dahl, Roald, *James and the Giant Peach*; Thomas, Dylan, *Under Milk Wood*, London, J. M. Dent & Sons, Ltd., 1956; Joyce, James, *Dubliners*; Lagerkvist, Par, *The Dwarf*; Kawabata, Yasunari, *The Master of Go*; Shakespeare, *The Sonnets*; Wodehouse, P. G., *Right Ho, Jeeves!*; *National Geographic World Atlas*, 8th edition; *1000 Years of Irish Poetry*; all of Agatha Christie, and an armful of Asimov.

This is how I'm growing up.

I know my mother never stopped buying books after my father died. It was his passion, I think, though my mother's a reader, too. She told me he would come home with boxes of books from library sales or garage sales, and he would sit up until all hours, reading the books, picking at them. Most he would keep; some he would give away again. "Such a mess," she said once. "But you ate them, too."

I was born with a book in my hand, she said. The haiku of Basho.

> Now I see her face,
> the old woman abandoned,
> the moon her only companion

Or:

In the moonlight a worm
silently
drills through a chestnut

I see the silent worm. It's like the wiggly, slippery thought that keeps me awake, right? I want to sleep but I can't. Worm. Worm.

And who is that old woman? She's a real woman, but she's also the old woman inside me who will be left by everyone. Why won't she die? Tick, tick, tick, tick. She's a watch that won't stop ticking, and she has to go on when all the other watches have died.

Purpose

THE REASON I'M ALIVE at all. How am I supposed to know? Only God knows. Maybe you know.

Maybe I'm meant to build bridges, cut tumors out of the brains of children, or find stars in the folds of space. I sometimes wonder if I'll die a hero, protecting the world or just one person from death, from fire or murder. Why else do I bleed if not for something big and rare? I look deeper, get quieter, trying to find what makes me want to live.

Confessions

THE SEVEN DEADLY SINS and the Seven Princes of Hell: Mammon, the demon of greed; Belphegor, the demon of sloth; Satan, the demon of anger; Beelzebub, the demon of gluttony; Lucifer, the demon of pride; Asmodeus, the demon of lust; and Leviathan, the demon of envy.

I think the money in another person's pocket is meant to be in mine.

Last week, a woman dropped her wallet on the sidewalk. I picked it up, and I wanted to take her money.

When I think of myself as a grown man, if I haven't made the vow of poverty, I'll live in a house where I can sit in an armchair looking over the world through a wide, wide window. I will listen to music playing from a very expensive stereo. I might want to make money without working. I'd own a big luxury car, one of those British kinds, a Bentley or Rolls-Royce, which would be like driving around in my living room.

Mammon rubs his hands.

I want to confess to the things that make me cry. I don't have to say why they make me cry. They just do. Music. Beauty. My headaches. Poverty. The hungry. The sick and crippled. The bullied. The grieving. The raped and murdered. My mother's loneliness. The impossibility of you. Haven't I made you up?

These things beat me up. They make me bleed, and they bruise me. My body hurts. Some days, because of all the pain, I beg my mother to let me stay in bed. I won't go to school. I won't get up until after noon. My body hurts. I know my legs will break if I try to stand. So I stay in bed, thinking, not even reading. I write poems. I cry. I sleep. I become one with the bed, rooted. I'm a sort of mushroom.

I've wanted to kill myself.

I can hear the crying, soothing Belphegor who lies down next to me and holds my eyes shut.

I want to confess to the things that make me angry. The men who stare at my mother like she's a steak dinner. Car horns. Sirens. Crowds. Going to school, even though I can basically do what I want when I'm there. The fact I cry so easily. Physical pain. My bleeding and my hidden purpose.

I get angry if I have to stand in line for any reason. Angry at people who leave their dogs tied up outside no matter what the weather is. Angry in the heat. Angry when people litter. Angry if I have to answer the phone while my cereal gets soggy in milk.

I get mad at babies who cry, but I also get mad at babies who laugh. Barking dogs. Lawn mowers. Leaf blowers. Current events. Past events. Future events, like the end of the world when our sun finally gets tired of it all and explodes.

It's bad enough I get angry at so much. I'm sure it's more.

It's how big my anger gets. Sometimes, it takes up all of me. My bones are made of anger, my veins and arteries, my eyes, my brain, my organs. Am I made from anger? It seems bigger than me, twice as big as me, and I want to crumple everything into a little ball, including myself, and throw it away. Satan commands it.

I've been known to eat until I make myself sick. I drink a gallon of milk every two days. I eat cereal by the bushel. I eat and eat and drink and drink. The whole time, Beelzebub snorts and burps.

Lucifer stands behind me. I have more intelligence, talent, physical strength, height, and speed than any other boy my age. You will know me as a king, a kind of god, able to do anything, think anything. Erik.

I can do anything except ask a girl out. So, Asmodeus, constantly licking his lips, and I have to watch Gemma Burns from far away. Her beauty and body make me dark, almost angry, and she stands under the arm of a false king, Sam McHugh.

Gemma isn't you. I know it. But I want Gemma to be mine, and for Sam to turn to sand. Green Leviathan roars.

Salve

THE SEVEN DEADLY SINS have their answer in the Seven Heavenly Virtues.

The woman dropped her wallet. I shouted, Ma'am, Ma'am, even though I could see the bills in their slot, feel the weight of the change, and I returned it, even though I wanted to run with it. The woman who dropped the wallet was old. She walked with a cane in one hand, and she might have lost the wallet from her other, trembling hand, or from her pocket. Her eyes were watery, and her mouth was folded in on itself. If I'd known at the beginning where this wallet came from, I would never have thought to run with it, to steal it for myself.

"Oh, how stupid," she said. "Careless."

I wanted to help her walk, but she limped off on her own, talking to herself.

I thought, *It shouldn't matter. I shouldn't steal from anyone, young or old, or pray for easy money.*

I can't claim all the credit for it, but I didn't hang myself or cut myself open in a tub. No matter how sad I get, or agitated, or storm-driven, I always do get up. I walk. I remember my mother. I remember you are in this world for me, and I am in this world for you. I remember whatever God might be, and I think about what has to get done. I have to do what's next on the list—go to school, help my mother, feed the hungry—and I have to do it awake.

I hear the sirens and the car horns, and I close my eyes and breathe.

The graying wolves see my mother as the alpha female, the one and only she-wolf who fed Romulus and Remus. She is that mythical and that beautiful. They can't help themselves. They're men. They lust. They're greedy, they're gluttonous, and my mother is a woman who attracts the best and worst in them. They want Rome. I know this, and I have to forgive them for their looks and comments and desires, even if I find nothing more insulting and dangerous. They want Rome.

I eat and eat, and I drink and drink, but I don't throw food away. The plates get licked clean. I finish everything, and my mother says I'm a growing boy. I feed the hungry at the shelter at St. Barnabas, and when I'm there, no matter how starving I am, I don't take a bite of food. I told my mother in a note, *No more sweet cereal.* I keep a fast between eight at night and seven the next morning. A long time ago, I gave up salt.

I love my mother. She reminds me that nobody is perfect. She tells me my father drank, sometimes too much, and they'd decided to face the problem together. Then he died. I wanted to ask if she thought he might have been drunk the afternoon he died, or if he'd ever ridden his bicycle with me after he'd been drinking, but I don't want to know.

I imagine the driver of the car who hit my father horrified when he saw a man on his bicycle wobbling or swerving out into the intersection without looking. The driver might not have been able to do a thing, all of it happening so fast. Can you see the grief? The real driver left the scene, but imagine getting out of a car and coming around front and seeing a full-sized man bleeding and gasping in the street, all but dead. I might throw up on the spot or start crying.

What last thought went through my father's mind? I'm sure, thinking of it now, he died in the street or in the ambulance. What was his last thought?

"Are all these bright lights for me?"

"Thank God Erik wasn't in the basket. You would've lost everything, Magda."

"I lost my hat. Has anyone seen my hat?"

"Cold."

"Sky."

I go to St. Barnabas. I know one or two of the men who get their meals there must have been the smartest and fastest and most talented boys at sixteen. A man named Kermit I've met only once, supposedly went to Yale Law at nineteen only to come here for his food. His daughter drowned. "And my son," he said, "he must be your age, but he's—. I don't know what to do about anything. I've lost my way."

The men at the kitchen have their stories and sadness, and I wonder if they suffer demons.

Gemma Burns cried on my shoulder when Sam McHugh forgot Valentine's Day. "I don't want to hear anything," she said. "I don't want to hear you say a word to me, and I know you won't. But you'll listen, and if I ask you, you'll write me a note. I know you're smart. Maybe I should always have been with you."

I dropped my head.

"I know you like me, Erik." She wore her hair in a bun so you could see her neck and shoulders, including the birthmark about three inches from her neck just below her collarbone. She's already a woman. I listened. She told her sad story of neglect, and I realized even the most beautiful girl can be left crying with the wrong guy.

I took out a piece of paper and a pen, and I wrote something like this. *We're young. Take a deep breath and go shine your light. Happy Valentine's Day.*

Gemma read the note. Then she asked a very, very good question: "Why don't I shine my light on you?"

I held my pen over the paper, shaking for what felt like a year. I thought about asking her to a movie. I imagined kissing her, and I wondered for a moment, a split second, if she could be you after all. I finally wrote. *Your light's too bright for me, Gemma. You're too glittery. You should be with a boy who talks, and every word he says should be your name.*

She took the note, read it, folded it carefully, and slid it into her white pleather purse. "Here's the problem with you," she said. "You just wrote the most amazing thing, the perfect thing. What girl doesn't want a compliment like that? But you're saying you won't have me. Or you think I won't have you." She shook her head at me: "You're so dumb. I don't understand you at all. You don't want me with Sam. I know you don't want that. All you have to do is take a walk with me or ask me to a movie. We could sit together without saying a word the whole time."

Gemma twisted the strap of her purse in her hands. "I talk enough for the two of us," she said. "But when I shut up, we'll kiss. You're the best-looking boy in school, even if you're the weirdest. What are the chances of that? The weirdest boy is also the smartest, biggest, and cutest. It's not like I haven't thought about you already. It's not like I don't wonder what you'd be like."

She took one more breath and sighed. "Nobody would mess with you if we went out together. You're huge and crazy."

Wait, I wrote. *Crazy?*

"Come on, Erik," she said. "You know you are. This can't be a surprise. It's part of what makes you you."

I shook my head and wrote, *I don't know if I'm crazy, but I can't figure out anything. I want to concentrate. That's all.*

"Concentrate on what?" Gemma said. "Whatever. I know you will. But before then, you should take me out."

I had to get away from her.

No, Gemma. I can't do that. I'm sorry. I have to go.

"You don't care who gets the light?" she called after me. "Even if it's Sam?"

I think what's most interesting about the Seven Deadlies and the Seven Heavenlies is that they all exist in each other. The Seven Sins mingle. The Seven Heavenlies mingle. But they stand on opposite sides of the room, like boys and girls at a sixth-grade dance, and can't stand to look at each other. I know what I'm talking about.

Some say the Deadlies start with Pride and the Heavenlies with Charity, with Love. It's true. If we put ourselves above everything else, we fall, we fall into anger and laziness and all the others. Love, nothing is harder than love, nothing wants or asks more from us. Love gives us everything that's good in us.

Which of the Deadlies is it hardest for me to avoid, and which of the Heavenlies is hardest for me to practice? Of the Sins, I'm angriest. This makes Satan happy. Patience has a tough time.

When will my anger go away? Nothing takes away from

it. It's infinite, but it doesn't belong to me. It was put into me in a locked garage by a man I might never see again, a man I might not even recognize if he stood right here, but it doesn't belong to me.

Anger. I know it will leave me the more I love.

I don't even know what that means, but I know it's true.

Footnote

GEMMA'S SEEING SAM AGAIN, and Sam looks the same as he did before. He's careless and smirking, but I have no right to judge. I have to turn away from Gemma, especially when she tries to catch my eye.

I have my blood and the promise of some fate, a fate that includes you. Right? You're a sure thing, yes?

Negative Space

I JUST WENT INTO the kitchen and poured myself a glass of milk, almost to the top. The glass might be five-sixths full. Above the white milk, there's the empty part of the glass.

Would anyone see the glass as one-sixth empty? If the glass were half full, would a person even find it possible at first glance to see it half empty? I mean, I look at the stuff that's in the glass, not the blankness of the other, empty part.

Right?

The invisibility of the one-sixth. I can see the edge of the glass, but even if the material is clear and nearly invisible, it's not negative. It exists. Glass is almost invisible, that's all. But birds die against windows. They fly right into the pane and crack their little heads. And dogs and people walk into sliding doors.

It's never funny when a bird dies against a window, but it's almost always funny when a person walks into a sliding door. Why?

Negative space. The space left inside and outside of the boundaries made by physical objects. This is a tough idea. I'm trying to get my head around it since I just read about it in an article in *Architectural Digest*.

If I make my arms into a circle, the space inside the circle is negative. It has shape but no substance. The space outside my arms, as marked by my face or any other object, would also have a shape, I guess, though harder to tell. When I stand with my legs apart, there's a triangle of negative space I make with the ground.

I can train my eyes to see negative space. It's hard to see it without practice.

Sorry, I have to go back to the glass.

Who would see the glass of milk I have right now as one-sixth empty? Would anyone see the empty space before seeing the filled space? If I poured an alcoholic half a glass of wine, would he only see the part of the glass that didn't have the wine? Would he see the glass half empty?

Sorry, sorry. I'm thinking.

Is the definition of a pessimist a person who only sees what he hasn't got but wants? Would an optimist never see the empty space?

Or is there some other detail I'm leaving out? Is it more complicated?

I don't know. It isn't always bad to see the empty space, is it? Isn't it all right to see both, the filled space and the empty space? You could be in either. I have to try and see everything.

Work

A FEW MONTHS AFTER my father died, I finally knew he was gone. The smell of his paints and turpentine once stained the air, stained his skin, my mother's hair, and my clothes. I grew up in the smell of his real work, and the smell was gone, disappeared. I went to the small room where he painted. There was an easel, a clean canvas, a stool speckled with paint and graffiti, a worktable, and a coffee can with brushes, pencils, and palette knives. I remember the folded easel against the wall, the canvas on the floor next to the easel, and the stool under the table. No rags, no tubes of paint. Diesel fumes from a passing bus came through the window. My father was gone.

My crying, red-nosed mother gave me an early birthday present. A small set of watercolors in an aluminum case and a pad of paper. I didn't want to open the case of paints, so my mother opened it for me. Inside were eight dishes of dry color, a brush, and an instruction booklet. My mother got a glass of water. She wet the brush and swirled the bristles in the yellow dish. A small pool of colored water formed on the surface. Then she opened the pad of paper and pulled the brush along the first page. When she handed me the brush, I shook my head. "Oh, Erik," she said. My poor mother. She lost her husband to a car, then she lost me to my first silence.

My father kept a set of miniature fired bricks on a bookshelf in his and my mother's bedroom. I must have first used the bricks with him, sitting on his lap at a card table or on the floor, but I don't remember it. One afternoon, I went into the bedroom to find the bricks. I had to stand on the bed to reach the shelf against the wall where the box sat. I had just enough strength to pull the set out, but not nearly enough to hold it. The box fell on my head and burst open. Most of the bricks fell across the mattress, but enough hit the floor to startle my mother.

"Erik, what are you doing?" She ran into the room and saw the bricks all over the blankets and floor. "Are you all right?" She took me close and looked me over. "You should've asked."

We got to the floor. "Papa loved these bricks," she said. "They were his, no doubt about it. He didn't let you play with them alone." After we collected all the bricks into the box, my mother carried them to my father's workroom. "You can build in here, Erik. Spread out."

I worked where my father worked, in the shadow of his table. I built towers. I built forts and castles. A few days went like this before I opened the easel and set up the canvas. I imagined my father at work with his oils while I sat with the hundreds of small red bricks. Hours I spent in that room, day after day. My mother stayed away, letting me work alone in the company of my dead father's tools. She announced meals to me through the door, and I would answer either by going to the table or not. She brought me snacks of apple slices and raisins. All along, I kept silent.

One morning, my mother knocked on the door to the workroom and let herself inside. "May I join you?" I turned back to the bricks, and my mother sat down. I remember she tied her unbelievable hair behind her head before getting to work. We built a fort. She got through an entire wall and tower by herself. How did she know how? Anyway, we worked side by side in silence together for days, maybe months and years. When we finished, she straightened herself.

"Ooh, this is murder on my back," she said. "But I think it's a great fort."

I swept my arm across it all, an angry little god, destroying it, and pushed the bricks aside. I started again.

Before I began painting the scene of my father's death, I worried he might get angry. What if he came back to paint his final subject? I must have known he wouldn't return. I used a new tin of paints my mother had given to me. Instead of the brush the set supplied, I picked one of my father's brushes from the coffee can. I found a jar on his table and filled it with water. I got to work.

I don't know how long I built with the bricks in the morning and painted in the afternoon. The painting looked more like a comic strip. I painted my father on his bicycle. I painted the park, as I imagined it, and blue skies with birds flying over the trees. I painted a skinny tree, dying of hunger. My father stopped at the weak tree. He talked to it and held its branches. Once the tree swallowed my father and his bicycle, it stood up fat and tall. I'd finished my first and last canvas.

What else could I do but find my mother and show her my work?

I worried I'd failed when she began to cry.

"Erik," she said, "talk to me. Won't you please talk to me?" She kneeled. "I miss Papa, but I miss you more now. Come back to me." My mother held me hard. I felt her strong arms across my back and her tears on my neck. My poor, poor mother. I tasted the sweat on her skin and felt the heat of her cheek.

I closed my eyes. Shadows came and wings spread. With the wings came the pain and noise.

"Mama," I said, "do you hear the train coming?"

Courtship

I SOMETIMES MISS MY mother. Since Lincoln the Gentle-man divorced his wife to capture my mother, I don't see much of her, or them. "You don't need me, really," she said. "You're too smart and independent to need anything from me."

They shower, they cuddle, they eat, they sleep, they walk, they talk. All of it together. Lincoln is good to me, a father. He always has a dollar, always listens. But he loves my mother. She'll be his true wife, so she comes first, as she should.

For us, since we'll happen so fast, we'll court each other after we're a done deal. Instead of a courtship that ends in marriage, we'll have a marriage that starts our courtship. We'll charm each other to keep what we have. We'll have a movie night once a week, a date night. We'll flip a coin to decide the theater, and we'll go after dinner. We'll get there whenever we get there and see what's playing next. No matter what the movie is, whether it's supposed to be good or terrible, we'll see it. We're there for the company and to make the best of it. We're there to turn off our brains and to hold hands in the dark. For two hours, we won't want to be anywhere else. Then we'll walk home.

Of course, to make this happen, we have to meet.

Size

MY MOTHER IS RIGHT. I don't need her much.

I've reached 6'9" and 225 pounds, no sign of stopping. I'm sixteen and a half. I've outgrown Martin the Irishman, who stopped at 6'5¾" and weighs about fifty pounds less.

You'd think I would play basketball, like Martin, or football. I've been recruited and recruited, but I want no part of it. Too violent, too aggressive, and I have no interest in hurting or getting hurt.

I found the perfect sport for me: rowing. After school once, I walked a long way around toward the subway home. A rowing team gliding over the river, perfect union, barely touching water, and I thought, *That's for me. Nothing else but that.*

Rowing has made me strong, almost stronger than Jacob, who wrestled with an angel. Or was it a man? Or was it God?

I want to row by myself in a single scull. The water, the oars, God, and me, in motion, inseparable, peaceful.

Matthew, Mark, and Luke

READING THE BIBLE ISN'T easy. It takes me a long time. Especially in the Latin, which is how I've been taking it, side by side with English. School Latin and nothing else.

I read every word because every word matters.

Maybe not every word, since I skipped over the genealogy of Jesus in Luke after reading it in Matthew. Mark leaves it out.

Anyway, I read almost every word, but I keep falling asleep. It's not that I get bored. All the talk of miracles and antichrist and betrayal and torture and death and resurrection, no, I don't find it boring. It tires me out. Concentrating wears me down.

Sometimes the words rise up off the page and dissolve, and sometimes the pages stick together with honey. I always smell flowers when I read.

Some languages are considered dead, like Kwadi, Esuma, Chorotega, Thracian, Etruscan, Assan, Mahican, and Beothuk. Experts say languages die every day, maybe tens of them.

Some nearly died. Irish came pretty close to the coffin. And others are kind of dead: Aramaic, Sanskrit, and Latin, which show up in various ways, though no one uses them day to day. I wouldn't recognize Aramaic if it bit me.

Latin, deadish, centuries of bad breath and coughing, still

serves the one book almost nobody on earth can seem to avoid, whether you visit a motel or live in the jungle, the book that may be the most alive: the Bible.

et respondens angelus dixit ei ego sum Gabrihel

intrate per angustam portam quia lata porta et spatiosa via quae ducit ad perditionem et multi sunt qui intrant per eam

exinde coepit Iesus ostendere discipulis suis quia oporteret eum ire Hierosolymam et multa pati a senioribus et scribis et principibus sacerdotum et occidi et tertia die resurgere

et perducunt illum in Golgotha locum quod est interpretatum Calvariae locus

Gabriel, the messenger angel.

Jesus describes the narrow gate of heaven and the wide gate of hell.

Jesus foretells His death and resurrection.

The Place of a Skull.

The Place of a Skull, where men and a god ended crucified. Crucified. I can't even wrap my pea brain around this. Nailed to a rough cross and left to hang until dead. Bleeding and broken and thirsty and hungry. What kind of mind thinks of this?

Matthew, Mark, and Luke. Who were they? Did they even exist? They couldn't have been the only people writing about Jesus. Why are they here and not others? Why aren't there six or twelve or twenty-four Gospels? Why no Gospel written by a woman? Or a sixteen-year-old boy? Jesus went about His Father's work when He was twelve, Luke says. By Father, he meant God.

Those first three Gospels, all miracles, disease, suffering, dirt, blindness, devils, blood, anger—so much anger—weakness, and mockery. Not much in the way of peace.

The miracles come again and again, like arrows. Arrow after arrow after arrow at His enemies.

The stories and parables, His stones.

Parable and Blood

"THE BUILDER AND THE OX"

A man in a town decided to build a stone house with the help of an ox. He quarried the fieldstone by himself. Imagine the geometry of the work: the parallel planes of sky and field; two arcs, the blade of a shovel and its cut in the dirt; a coiled rope; a taut rope; the oblong muscles in his grinding jaw and the shape of each creaking tooth; the slope of his back; a triangle, the arches of his feet and the center of his skull its vertices; the iron globe of his heart.

The town said, "Why would you do this by yourself? So much work when you can have a house put up in a day with our help?"

"What can I say?" the builder said. "A voice told me this is the house I have to build and the way I have to build it."

The town went away dissatisfied with the answer, grumbling to itself, but it left the builder alone with his work.

The builder devised a wooden staging to go up with each story. He built a treadmill on the staging for the ox to work lifting the stones into place. Early on, he tried to catch a falling stone and lost two fingers of his right hand, cracked and pulped as if between a giant's molars. He suffered little else other than a broken toe, caught beneath the hoof of his sidestepping ox.

One year from the first sight of buried rock, the man and his ox set the final stone. The rest of the town turned out to witness the end of his solitary work. The ox turned the wheel; the ropes snapped and quivered; stones rubbed.

His work ended here.

The man skimmed mortar from the edge of his trowel with his thumbnail. The town watched him rub the flat blade. A single handclap sounded. This collision of hands, like a collision of flint, threw a spark. Another man caught fire and went up in applause. Each clap was a flying, popping ember; fire consumed the crowd. An ovation blazed.

The town celebrated and grew hungry. Once unyoked, the tireless ox was slaughtered on the staging, its meat roasted and divided among the people. The builder himself requested a portion from the blackened shoulder. He sweat ox blood as he ate. The blood stained his temples and ears.

I'm glad I don't have to explain this. I take my lead from Jesus. He never explained His parables.

I'm bleeding. It stains my temples and ears.

As far as I know, this is my last miracle. Nothing else.

John

JESUS WEEPS FOR LAZARUS. Out of His sadness, out of His love, and with all the power of God behind Him, He raises Lazarus from the dead. He calls a man dead four days out of his grave. This more than anything else gives Jesus His enemies. No one likes a show-off. The cross was a matter of time.

What's the lesson? Did sadness and love allow Him to be nailed up? Or did anger and revulsion force the hammering?

ecce homo: Behold the man.

mandatum novum do vobis ut diligatis invicem sicut dilexi vos ut et vos diligatis invicem

This means, in my translation of a translation, "I'm giving you an order, okay? Right now, a new one. Love each other. Love each other like I've loved you."

Yes. I'll try. I will always try, even if it makes me sad, gives me headaches. Even if it crucifies me. I have to remind myself, the crucifixion might be a relief.

You see? Sometimes I think I've given up on you. Can you feel this? Maybe I lied to myself about you. I ask myself over and over again, *What's her name? What's her name?*

Stupid. I have no real reason to think you exist. I could be wasting time. Normal people have more than one girlfriend and even more than one wife. Why should I wait?

I tell myself to wait because you'll make everything worth-while. I tell myself it's okay to be lonely and to suffer and bleed because you'll solve everything. I can't be the only person on earth to go through life like this. I'm not utterly alone. There are others like me. You're like me.

Brothers

"I'M NOT SURE IF you would be friends or enemies." The man from the Barnabas kitchen, Kermit, with one dead daughter and one living son, was talking. "I wouldn't want to have an enemy your size, but I can't say my son would choose to be your friend. He's not at a soup kitchen. I'm not sure where he is. Or maybe it's me. I haven't been home in a while." He swallowed a chunk of bread. "You don't talk. The silent type. He is, too. Maybe you'd sit together without a word between you. I'm thinking it'd be more for him than for you. He'll soak up your gentleness. I frankly don't know what you'd get in the bargain. We can't choose our brothers."

I nodded and shrugged, and he took my arm. "He may never come here, but you'll have to meet sometime, somewhere. I'm sure of it. Or maybe I want it for him. I don't know. You two are marked for each other."

Even if I'd wanted to speak, what could I have said? There's only one person I'm destined to meet. A wife, not a brother.

Frustration

WHO GUIDES ME? WHAT?

I walk, read, think, write, and row. Is this a purpose? This is my to-do list.

What is being prepared for me? Tell me. Tell me.

Why?

GOD GIVES US MYSTERIES to solve. Most of the time, these mysteries have to do with other people. Why do people steal from their mothers, murder children, burn down houses, sell drugs, rape, bomb markets, bulldoze forests, and hit men on bicycles with their cars and drive away? Why do people fight fires, enlist in the armed forces, chase muggers, become brain surgeons or monks, sell flowers, or teach eighth grade?

Some people have a meaning we can't figure out. They show up in our lives from the mind of a god, out of thin air, they stay for a little while, they show us our life, its future or present, and then they disappear. They fall through a drain. They burst into flames. They starve themselves. They walk away. A disease takes them. They die.

Joan

THE THOUGHT OF JOAN makes me want to sleep. What else should I do? I get so sad. I thought for sure you came as Joan. I thought your name was Joan. I was wrong.

Spring, and I'd just finished my last final. I stood on the train platform during rush hour, shifting my weight from one foot to the other, waiting for the uptown express. Normally, I'd have chosen to walk rather than take a train or bus, especially when I felt restless, but I had to make a rowing practice. I'd already learned how to be gentle with a boat, but I was still getting strong. I looked along the steel tracks for the light of a train hurtling through the tunnel. Nothing.

That's when I noticed a girl reading a plain white paperback. She seemed too thin to be real, the silhouette of a girl projected onto a column. I couldn't see her face behind her hair. The train pulled into the station, and the girl stuffed her book in her bag. She hooked her auburn hair behind her ear, and I thought I recognized her. The face I once saw in my winter breath, almost transparent, ghostly.

You?

The train, brakes screaming, slid to a stop, and I hurried toward the girl. I'm tall and strong, so I could push through the crowd. People told me to watch it, but I ignored them. I wanted to get on the train with the girl. When the doors closed behind me, I looked up. She stood facing me, but there was a man, a wall between us, and he smelled of sweat and hair gel. I hated him. I looked at the girl's face. She was in college, I thought, eighteen or nineteen. She had different-colored eyes, one blue and one brown, unreadable, and a short, fine nose. Her thinness—. Her flower-print tank top and blue jeans gave her presence; otherwise, she might not have been there at all. She caught me looking at her, and I turned away, ashamed and frightened. I know how tempted I am by the impossible.

When I dared to look at her again, she was reading her book. The title of it was in French, *La symphonie pastorale*.

The train lurched. I hadn't noticed it stopped between stations. It pulled into the next station, brakes squealing and squealing, and I wondered if the girl would get off. She didn't. Neither did the man between us, and there was no room to move. The train shuddered, bucked into motion, and the girl, who was turning a page, lost her balance. She would've fallen into the woman on her right if I hadn't put out my arm, knocking the man in front of me. I caught the girl by the shoulder, and she said, "Oh." Her shoulder was small and soft in my hand. I thought I'd hurt her, and I pulled back. Her frailty vanished, leaving an emptiness in the middle of my palm, an emptiness heavier than the weight of her body. I could see the imprint of my thumb in her skin, like a burn.

"All right?" I said, ashamed by my brutishness.

"Yes," she said, recovering. "You've got quick reflexes."

The man who smelled of sweat and gel sighed audibly and jerked his shoulder, as if from an unwanted touch.

The rest of the way, I couldn't look at her again. I hated myself. I felt stupid and oafish. Here was the girl I once saw in my breath—I still thought it was you—and I'd hurt her. She had skin soft as my breath. I was rough and stupid: I couldn't touch a girl; I couldn't take care of a fragile thing. Like Lenny from *Of Mice and Men*. I wanted off the train. If only I could've opened the doors then and there, the train in motion, and jumped out onto the tracks, escaped into the tunnel. I'd had thoughts of talking with her, but now I was glad for the wall of a man between us.

The train rolled into the station. I couldn't stay on a moment longer. I faced the doors and put my hand up against the glass. My hand was huge, an animal's paw, a bear's paw.

The doors opened.

I took the stairs at a run. Up, up, up I ran, into the perfect intelligence of sunlight and loneliness.

Except I wasn't alone.

Wait. Where are you running off to?

How could she—? Her voice came from inside.

Stop running. Stop. Turn around.

I turned around, and there she stood, not even out of breath, coming off the stairs to the subway. *Why did you run away?* Her voice still in my head. Did her lips move?

"I thought—. How'd you follow me so fast?"

I flew.

I believed her.

What's your name, giant?

"Erik."

"Erik?" She spoke out loud suddenly, excited. "Thorvalds-son?"

"Thorvald—?"

"The Viking murderer and explorer. Father of Leif."

"Lynch. But I always wanted to be a Viking."

You look like him, all coppery and shining.

"What's your name?"

Joan. Walk with me, Erik Lynch.

"I can't. I'm on my way to the boathouse."

"I know." Out loud again. "Walk with me, instead."

"I—"

"Haven't you been watching? Haven't you seen me? I'm dying."

Silence.

"I didn't want to think—"

"You can't avoid it. Walk with me."

"Okay." She took my hand. Hers was so fragile, like a leaf. "What do I say?"

"We'll walk for a while, sit in a park, and then we'll say good-bye. I think I have a handkerchief. I'll clean up your blood a little."

"My blood."

"Yes, your stigmata. Then we might kiss. After everything, you'll think about me for the rest of your life. I'll be dead in a month or so, maybe six weeks. But we won't see each other again. I won't tell you where I am. I won't tell you my last name. I'll be the wife who'll never be your wife."

At that moment, I knew, I knew for sure, she couldn't be you. She said all the right things, but—. How could you die before we lived? Impossible.

"You can't be my wife."

"I mean—"

"I know what you mean. If you'd survive whatever's killing you, then, maybe."

"Walk with me."

"You're just going to leave me sad."

"No, I won't. Erik, come with me."

We walked. It doesn't matter what we said or where we went. I pretended for a little while she was you. We kissed, and when we kissed, the world flipped downside up. I picked her up in my arms, and she laughed. "Put me down."

"You don't weigh anything."

"I'm almost dead, and this is the sweetest thing anyone has ever done for me." We sat down on a bench. "Witness," she said, crying. "You're my witness."

I nodded, and she let out a deep sigh.

"Would you do me a favor?"

"Yes."

"Hold me. Until the crying stops."

I cradled her, and one of us groaned. You'd think I'd lifted a tree instead of a dying girl. Everything felt heavy. All the silence. I shook. I could hardly take her weight. I pressed her nose and mouth against my shoulder and snuffed out the sound of her weeping.

Fate

I'M CONVINCED I'LL DIE young. I wonder if even you could help keep me alive. My father died surrounded by all my mother's beauty and love. True love doesn't prevent death. I used to think it did.

I've got my invisible wounds. I can't stop bleeding.

I give blood for blood, and I'll be dead before I'm twenty. For me, the sky and earth are the same. There's no division, no horizon. I'm always walking in fog and mud. I have no idea where I'm going, but I'm going straight, straight toward the center and straight away from it. There's no east or west or north or south. There's only one direction. You and death, in that order. I can almost touch you, and you're as far as the South Pole. I'm a clown and a genius. I'm alive and as good as dead.

At the moment I die, everything will clear up. The sky and ground will separate. I'll hear your voice. I'll carry a man out of a fire or save a child from drowning. All done.

Finally, I get it. I understand. I'll die, and you'll have to find another husband. You'll be too young to go without love for the rest of your life. You'll have two husbands. I'll only be the first.

I don't think I've ever been sadder than I am right now.

THORN

WHEN I WAS TEN, Kulthat and Tillion drove me to the hospital. They told me if I didn't calm down, they'd leave me there forever. I had my knapsack. I was screaming. Screaming and screaming. I wouldn't stop. My father had put out ten cigarettes in my legs, and they were sticking up like little smokestacks. Why did he do that? He denied it of course. He said, I did no such thing. Never, never. The liar. Liar. Like I'd make that up. People are always making things up, but not me, not me. I tell the truth always.

You'll stay here, my demon parents told me. You'll stay here if you don't calm down. This place is meant for you. Hell. Gehenna.

I stopped my screaming, and they took me home.

But what if I had kept on screaming? What if I'd been left at the hospital? How much worse could it have been?

Hirsute, that's the word. I'm hirsute. Which, according to the dictionary, makes me horrid. One archaic use of horrid means shaggy, bristling, rough. Horrid also means shockingly dreadful. Abominable. Hateful.

My hairline starts right above my eyebrows. My beard starts right below my eyes and grows south all the way to the bottom of my throat. I look like a monkey, though no tail, which makes me more ape. A skinny ape, runt ape, a laughingstock in a troop.

My girlfriend likes me, though. Candace. How I ended up with a girl named Candace I don't know. The name suits a girl or woman of a particular type. Classy, elegant. I'm not saying my Candace isn't classy and elegant. She is in her own way, boots and all, but she's no princess.

"I don't want to be a princess," she'd say.

"You don't have to be."

"Good, because I don't want to be. I'd rather be an expert in apes, live with apes my whole life. I'm practicing with you."

I let her shave my face now and then. At her house, in her family's bathroom.

"I always have to clean up super well. If my parents see little hairs all over the counter, they'll wonder where the hell they came from."

"Tell them they're mine. I had to shave for the tenth time in one day. They'd believe that."

"They would, but why here? They still don't think we're together."

"They never will. To them I'm nice enough but crazy."

"I'd say that's just about what everyone thinks, sweetie."

◇

In the Bible, Esau is born red and hairy and loses his birthright as firstborn to his twin, Jacob. And Jacob says, My brother is a hairy man, and I am a smooth man. They weren't identical twins. Fraternal.

I have no twin, fraternal or otherwise. I am a son, but no birthright will come to me. My father has finally left me alone. My mother, too. She committed suicide seven months ago.

◇

I found her. Hanging. She strangled herself with a brown six-foot extension cord. The one she'd connected to her iron.

Everyone asks: Was there a note? We always want explanations for the terrible things. Yes, a note. Three sentences. Very short sentences.

Good-bye, Kermit.

Good-bye, Hawthorn.

Good-bye, Salome.

◇

No explanation. No confession. No peace. Simply done.

◇

This left my father weak and distant. He had no strength to beat me, no energy for torture.

Once, a few weeks after my mother's death, Kulthat came

out of his hell and slipped while running after me. He fell like he was hit by a hammer. There he lay, on the floor. The sole of his foot facing the ceiling.

"Hawthorn, help me." My father's voice. In pain. No more Kulthat.

For the first time, I shuddered. A spasm like I'd been struck by a splinter of lightning. Not a full bolt. My head spun, every muscle clenched tight. My tongue between my teeth. No sound but a growl like thunder coming from somewhere inside of me. The Guardians.

My father held his shin and blubbered, so I kicked his foot. Not hard. A little tap, but he screamed. I kicked him harder, and his foot tipped toward the floor. He screamed.

"All the years," I said. "Eleven years."

I tugged his foot around so that at least it pointed in the right direction. My father stopped screaming and passed out.

◇

A month after my tiny revenge, my father limped away. I haven't seen him since. When have I been better off than now?

Did he suffer enough? His first child drowned. His wife committed suicide. His son hated him. That's a lot of pain. But I don't think he suffered enough for what he did to me.

◇

Sometimes having a girlfriend means wondering how long you'll have a girlfriend. I'm ugly. I know I am. Ugly outside, ugly inside. Girls don't dream of boys like me. Covered in hair, angry, easily upset. Why would a girl want this? Every night, just as I fall asleep, I wonder if I'll have a girlfriend when I wake up. Everything can change that fast, overnight. I could be left with less than nothing. Everything burned.

So I ask Candace occasionally, "How long will we have?"

"It's never good when you ask this. It means you're worried."

"Just answer. How long will we have together?"

"Until the very last moment."

"What does that mean? It could end right now." The Guardians, already angry, always angry I've let Candace so close for so long, wake up a little. I hear them in my voice. "You could snap your fingers this second. Is that what you mean?"

"You sound rough, Thorn. You have your demon voice."

"You said, 'Until the very last moment.'"

Candace puts her hand on my face, or on my shoulder. She might even kiss my cheek. She's nothing if not fearless. "I mean the very last moment we have on this planet. Together."

"How can you know that?" I'm angrier and angrier. My Guardians mobilize the Sawmen. Pain gets closer. "You don't love me. Who could love this?"

"I could," Candace says. "I do. Please calm down. We were having a good time."

The saws bite, and I'm done. Doubled over. Crying. Harmless.

◇

When I kicked my father's foot, I tortured him.

There are entire museums dedicated to the history of torture. There are men and women tortured today, right now, this second. The methods would give anyone nightmares. Anyone. Death would be a relief. Like aspirin or sleep.

I can hear my own bones breaking, my own muscles pulled out of my body, and I scream, "Kill me, kill me, kill me."

I've already known what it feels like, this kind of pain. I know what it means to want to die from pain. The pain my mother and father, Kulthat and Tillion, gave me. Plus, the Sawmen. The pain and fear from loving Candace. Kill me.

◇

I miss my mother. I miss Tatiana. Shouldn't we all have our mothers, so long as they aren't out to kill us?

A year ago, my mother left hell. We talked for a few months. We laughed and found a way to be together. We had an understanding. We wouldn't mention Salome's name. We wouldn't talk about the violence and punishment and war-fare between us. I would do this in return for dinner.

◇

Now I feed myself. Ten months, no mother. Eight, no father. I go to high school part-time, at night. I go at night, since I work thirty-two hours a week at Only a Game. Most days and every other weekend.

Along with math and chemistry, I take a course in creative writing. We got an assignment: Six-Word Stories:

The fever broke. We finally slept.

We prayed for rain or death.

◇

Only a Game. I mostly work with the board games, the games of strategy, and chess. I'm sort of a specialist. We're in a golden age of board games. New ones come out all the time. Some take an hour to play; others take days. Everybody's caught up in video games, but the tabletop is where it's at. For some of us. We're old-school.

The store has a whole section devoted to video games, of course. I see the kids and men, almost always boys and men, barely any girls, checking out the first-person-shooter games. I know what those games are, but I don't understand them. When you play board games, you learn about your mind and other people's minds. You find out whether or not you take risks, whether or not you're a short- or long-range thinker, whether or not you like to wager.

But in those shooter games, there's only one way to go. You can only go forward. Killing. There's nothing to learn. No thinking. It's some lower level of mind, instinct. You don't have to talk. The game gives you all the noise.

I played one of them. Once. After closing. A hired assassin. It went like a bad night's sleep. Shooting. Strangling. Stabbing. Kicking a man to death. Gunfire and grunts and wailing. Four hours gone in death. I died over and over. Other people died. Blood and broken bodies. The noise of it. When I stopped, I could barely stand up. I got sick.

Everything around me looked like a cartoon. Brighter colors. Sharper sounds. I was a five-and-a-half-foot length of live copper wire. I wanted to sleep, but I was shaking. Shuddering. Lightning. I sensed the Protector just under my skin, watching for danger, expecting a fight. I wanted to cry, so I did. I cried. I hated myself.

Is this what it's like in real life? Killing, I mean. The fear, the suspense, the sickness, the ease of it?

◇

I don't know. Maybe I'm wrong. Maybe a person can learn something from those games, like whether or not you think you have the stomach to kill another person.

Could I have killed my father when he was lying on the

floor that day his foot nearly snapped off? He was helpless. I hated him. If I were a hit man, he would've been dead in seconds. I didn't want him dead. I wanted him to suffer. There's a difference.

Could I ever see myself killing someone? If not my father, anybody? Maybe if I had to save someone else. Maybe if I had to protect myself. Maybe if I had to protect the world against evil. Otherwise, no.

Wait. Does killing someone include killing myself? Do I count?

◇

What am I talking about? I play chess. It's a field of battle. People die. I sacrifice my soldiers. And those strategy games? I kill all the time.

But I'm old-school. The killing I do doesn't look like killing, or even pretend to look like killing. I play quiet games. I have to think everything through.

◇

Wow.

I'm even uglier than I thought. Just like that. I'm worse than those first-person shooters, playing assassin. Worse than almost everybody in a new way.

I plan my killings. Premeditate. Pawn, knight, bishop, rook.

◇

"I don't know." Candace crossed her arms and looked around my apartment for the first time. I'd never brought her here, but my parents were gone. They left everything behind. "I don't know. It feels empty."

"Everything's here."

"I can see that, but it feels empty."

I tried kissing her, and she pulled away. Why would she do that?

"Something's not right." She started looking all over the house. "Do you even have parents?"

Why would she pull away? Is this the beginning of the end? It must be. It must be. I shuddered. That same jolt of electricity. It comes when I'm somehow scared or suspicious. The Guardians, or the Architect himself, I think, prodding me, telling me to be careful, to think.

There's only one reason to pull away from a kiss. You don't want to be kissed.

"I saw that, Thorn. The spasm. It's happening more and more."

"I know," I growled.

"Don't get angry with me. Do you have parents, yes or no?"

"Why would you ask such a question? Of course I have parents. Kiss me."

"No. I'm thinking." Candace picked up my mother's iron from the board in the hall.

"Don't."

"It's just an iron."

"My mother would kill me if it broke."

"Oh." Candace put it down on the board. "Like I'll drop it."

Why won't she kiss me?

"Why won't you kiss me?"

"Stop worrying. You always worry. Soon as you don't get what you want, you worry. Like I'm always pushing you away, right? Like I have someone else."

"Do you?"

"You see? You always get like this."

"Not always."

"Always." She wasn't even looking at me. By now, she was looking at Kermit's and Tatiana's bookshelves in their room. "I've never seen so many books on chess. Mom or dad?"

"My father."

"What's his name?" She pulled out a book and fingered through it.

"Don't." I was getting angry, but something in me wanted her to know everything.

"What's his name, Thorn?"

"Joseph."

"And your mom?"

"Mary."

"Very New Testament."

"I can't help that."

"So why does this book say, 'To Kermit, Happy Anniversary, I love you. Tatiana'?"

"It's used. Why won't you kiss me?"

She brought the book over.

"Except it's signed '*We* love you. Tatiana, Salome, and Thorn.'"

"—"

"Salome. Your dead sister."

"Don't say her—"

"You lied. Why would you lie?" She snapped the book shut. "And, really? Kermit, Tatiana, Salome, and Thorn?"

"Don't say her name."

"It's all weirdly beautiful. But why lie?"

"I can't tell you that yet."

"Yet? Why not?" She sat on the end of the bed.

"I'm not ready."

"I know you play chess." She flopped back on the bed.

"You're so beautiful." Why won't she kiss me? What does she want? Who does she want? Suspicion. The Sawmen were cutting.

"Sometimes, you look at me with your hand on your face, staring at me, like you're wondering what your next move should be."

"No I don't."

She laughed. "Yes you do. It's intense and stupid."

"Why stupid?" I stood there, stupid. "You should kiss me."

"Because there's only one move. And you're looking down on me, just like that. Again."

By now, I was so nervous, angry, and suspicious. Desperate. I didn't know what to do. The Sawmen halfway through my stomach.

"Zugzwang." The Architect was angry. The Guardians. The Sawmen. Everybody in motion. Everybody. All moving.

"What?" Candace sat up.

"Time to get out of here." I pulled her up by her arm. "Time for all of us to get out of here."

◇

Liar. Liar. Why won't you kiss me? Why won't you be honest? Liar. Liar.

I know your kind. I've known your kind my whole life. Liar. Liar.

◇

I have dreams. Long, frightening dreams. Last night I dreamed of a scaffold. Not a wood scaffold. Nothing simple like my mother swinging in a tiny circle. A man was the scaffold. That's all I can say. He was huge. He held me up. Another man would beat me until he got tired, but the scaffold wouldn't let go. He held me up and didn't say a word.

◇

What's the interpretation? Only one. My conscience held me up and beat the hell out of me. Why? Because I told Candace I wouldn't talk to her again? Because I told her not to look at me? If she sees me on her side of the street, cross it. If she sees me anywhere in the world, hide.

◇

Or was the scaffold the devil, and my father the demon that beat me?

No. There is only one interpretation.

Here's the problem with the ending between Candace and me. I don't think I'll ever meet another girl who likes me the way Candace did. I'll never touch another girl. I'll die before that happens.

◇

I'm back to shaving myself. It takes me nearly half an hour. I ask myself, Why not get an electric razor? So far I've been too stupid to know why.

I will let the beard go for a couple weeks. I don't care. By that time, I'll look like a wolf. I have large eyes. There they are. Bright blue shining out of a black beard, black eyebrows, and black curly hair. They burn through the dark. I sound like Superman, except his terrible little brother. A dwarf. Something dark and twisted in his supersoul. Hidden away. In the ice of the Fortress of Solitude. I'd wait for

Superman to come home, and I'd yell at him. I'd dance on his head like a monkey.

"How could you love them? How could you save them? Why couldn't you let them all die?"

"I have to love them and save them."

"You make me sick." I'd pretend to throw up on the ice.

"Love is the hardest thing of all to do. Faster than a speeding bullet? Stronger than a locomotive? That's just like breathing. But love? Love is worse than Kryptonite."

What can I say to that? The son of a bitch would be right.

◇

You people. You people. Youpeopleyoupeopleyoupeople. Cowards, every one of you. What, what, what, what keeps your legs from breaking under all the weight of your fear and lies and hatred? Human beings. I'm not one of you. I'm not one of you. I'm outside your fences. I'm running around you at the speed of light, you goddamn beasts. But you think I'm the monster. You cry and gnash your teeth. You throw stones at each other, at me, and you expect mercy all the time. You harm and harm and harm, and your lips turn blue and your teeth red and your eyes yellow and your skin green, and you bring down your swords, tear up each other's skin, throw your stones, and I run around you. But I'm the monster. I'm the goddamn monster. Alone.

◇

You see, you see, you see? I feel the Guardians. All their rage.

I want to be human. You're not all hateful cowards. I know that.

I'm turning into a monster or a ghost, I don't know which.

I don't want to be angry anymore. Or protected, if it means I feel this way, speak this way, and get sawn in half. That's the end result of the anger and protection: I get sawn up.

Don't be one of them, the Guardians say. *Stay with us. If you stay with us, we won't need to saw you. You'll be safe.*

I'm not safe with you, I can argue, or in the world. Where will I be safe?

I'm very, very sad, and very, very tired.

◇

Three words. First-person shooter.

◇

. . . and the entire world shades of purple. I don't know the names of more than one purple, lavender, so the world in shades of lavender, dark, light, black lavender, red lavender, blood lavender, all the trees, all the trees, dropping their purple leaves, and all the houses on every block wiggling and purple, like they're all mirages, the grass spikes of bright lavender, lightning lavender, cracking under my feet like icicles. Where's Candace now? Where's Candace now?

Where's Candace now? Liar, she's sitting in a coffee shop with her new boyfriend, laughing at me. They're laughing at me, because I'm ridiculous. Right? Right? Ridiculous, crazy, sad. So sad. Dead sister, dead mother, a father better off dead, finally gone. Only gone. Only gone. Only a game. First-person shooter. Bam. The lavender world, a headache. The Guardians say, *This is our world, buddy-boy. This is the color of our world. Take it, take it.* Where's Candace now? I'll walk until I find her. When did I stop sleeping? Days ago. Maybe naps like a purple cat, curled up in the purple sun. Pigeons. Pigeons. Pigeons and cats, a war between them, and both die by the dozen, pecked or clawed, pigeon blood, cat blood, everything terrible. I want to cry over the cats, not the pigeons. The pigeons that follow me, gurgle monsters. Gurgle monsters, they want to kill my hands. I haven't slept a full night for more than a week. I can't. I can't sleep, up, up, up, up, and I can't stop thinking.

All I want to do is walk. Walk and walk, miles and miles. One end of the city to the other, and one side to the other, and then all the middles, all the circles. I want to get beaten up, mugged, killed, killed, killed. Where's Candace? If she loved me, she'd be here now. She'd tell me nothing's purple, she'd tell me the houses shake and wiggle because I haven't slept, and she'd send me to bed and get me toast and ginger ale until I died. I'll walk and find her, if I have to go to every coffee shop in the city. *We were right*, the Guardians say. *We were right. You trusted a human being, and look where that got you. You deserve the saws, all the saws.*

I hear Candace and her boyfriend kissing. I hear them, explosions between them, I can hear them, all the kisses. Their tiny explosions. Like gunshots. POP. POP. POP. I see them in my apartment right now, my apartment now, dead mother, father gone, and they're in my mother's bed. I'll go home and find them, and he'll stand up, naked, and confront me. I'll break his arm. I'll make him eat his hand. When Candace screams, I'll say, You shut up and stay where you are. Do not make a move. Not a move, until I'm done with him. After he's swallowed his hand, I'll break his feet. You're not going anywhere. Then, I'll turn to Candace, and I'll say, Why? Why? Why? Why? Why? Why? Why?

That's not where they are. Why go to the monster's lair? No, they're somewhere, laughing and kissing. POP. POP. POP. Make it stop. Make it stop. Candace, please bring me ginger ale and toast. I'll sleep. I promise, I promise. Take me out of the purple world.

So I walk, and walk, and walk. I'm not worth my shoes, and the pigeons know this, but the cats kill them, feathers everywhere, bird bones breaking in their mouths.

Lavender. Black lavender teeth. You stop smiling at me. Stop smiling at me. I see your teeth, black lavender.

Candace? Ginger ale. Toast.

◇

Screaming. Like these cats, these armies of cats. The armies of pigeons are silent except for that low sound they make in their throats. What are they called, those sounds? What?

Hospital.

I need a hospital.

Where else can I go?

◇

Where are you, Candace? Where are you? Ginger ale and toast, toast and ginger ale. All of it the colors they're supposed to be. Hospital. The halls are triangular and wiggling like the lavender houses. These halls bright white lavender. Make it stop. Read the signs. Read the signs.

We're against this. The Guardians speaking. *We're against this.* The Sawmen go to work. Help me. They're here. I'm bleeding all over the floors, and I slip in my own blood, splash in puddles of my own blood, and then I'm healed, and I can stand up, get my balance, the blood gone, until the sawing comes again. *We're against this. We're against this.*

Emergency reception. Two nurses laughing with a man. Don't they see me? I'm invisible. Invisible as my saws. We're against this. Ginger ale. Toast. Not rye, not wheat, not white. Pumpernickel. Pumpernickel toast and soda forever. Yes, Candace. Yes, Candace. I'll sleep. Don't these people see me? A guard over my shoulder. Why? Going to hurt me? I'll bury that gun in his ear. Then I'll pull the trigger. First-person shooter. Only a game. That's where I work. Only a Game. I won't be there today. Don't these people see me? They're laughing and laughing.

◇

Out on the street. Walking. A park, a path, a tree. Sobbing. Sobbing all over. Crying and crying, so I can barely breathe. Watering the tree, making it grow. Salty leaves. Salt every-where. Salt drifts, saltmen, salt forts, saltball fights. Storms of salt, drowning cats and pigeons, pigeons forced out of the sky, saltfall, so hard. Sobbing that much. Can't stop. Where are you? Candace? Please, just some ginger ale and toast, and I'll sleep right here.

◇

A bad day. I have to get home. Six miles? I can do this. I'm not crying anymore. I'm not sleeping against a tree. I can walk and go home and sleep. I'm better now. Except for the saws, I'm fine. I have to walk.

◇

I'll buy some ginger ale and pumpernickel and butter. I'll be fine. Just get home.

◇

I can't eat. I can't drink.

Sleep. I can't sleep.

◇

Yesterday. A bad day. I feel as if I had my ass kicked. Everything hurts. All the energy taken up by a day like that. Every muscle fighting itself.

Here I am at home. Ginger ale, butter, pumpernickel. I don't even like pumpernickel.

◇

What did I do? Where did I go? I remember the hospital. I remember crying. I remember everything was purple. I must have bought soda and bread and butter. I don't remember doing it. I remember the saws. Nothing else.

Is it worth remembering?

EIGHTEEN

Your life is shaped by the end you live for.
You are made in the image of what you desire.

—Thomas Merton, *Thoughts in Solitude*

ERIK

The Beginning of the End

I'VE WALKED THIS CITY enough. I've walked it enough for two people. So what? I know nothing, I understand nothing. I sit on park benches and rest next to lunatics. Bar-bar-bar-bar-Barbara Ann. Not so long ago, a man asked me if Jerry Lewis had died, whoever that is. He wasn't too sure Jerry Lewis had died, so he wanted confirmation, a crucial want, it seemed to me. One man read the Bible aloud, even though he held it upside down.

I walk and walk. What else am I supposed to do? I'm asking you, if you exist. Anyone? What am I supposed to do?

I'm still bleeding, the stigmata: for what? Four years of blood only I can see. Oh, right, Joan saw my wounds. I forgot. Did she even exist? I mean, did that girl from the train even come up out of the station, out from underground? You would see me. I know you would.

I don't really care about anything. I write only to you. I don't read. I hardly think. I've given up on silence, on Latin, on the Bible, on rowing, on everything.

Miracles and impossibilities. What about it? What if I bend over to tie my shoe a sane person and stand up completely insane, no idea of who or what or where I am, screaming and howling? Who will be strong enough to calm me down? Who won't be in harm's way? Who will put me in the hospital for the rest of my life?

You can't help me. I've lost myself. I've lost the way I never had. You're nowhere to be found. Not yet. And I'm running out of time.

Reduction

TO FIND OUT WHAT I am, what I am supposed to do.

This is it. One purpose. If I didn't want so much to know why I'm here, on this planet, I would throw myself off the end of the world, out to the shadows.

I'm a hero in search of a disaster. I'm a martyr waiting for my holy death.

Height

I'M TIRED, SICK AND tired, of my size. Why would anyone in the world who's not a basketball player need to be seven feet tall? Unless you're Goliath, unless you're a soldier or a killer. Then, you'd strike fear in your enemies. There's no guarantee you'd survive the fight, though.

How tall are you? Every day, I have new reason to think you're an impossibility. I mean, what kind of a woman will want me, all seven feet of me and bleeding? You're an impossibility because I'm an impossibility.

I don't know when, a month ago, I ran into Gemma Burns on the street. I almost knocked her down. She looked up at me, and I looked down at her.

"Erik?"

"Gemma."

"You're talking." She took a step or two back, better to see my face. "You're huge. How tall—?"

"Too tall."

"You're unbelievable."

"How do you mean?"

"Look at you. You're—"

"It's been a couple of years."

"We, my family—." She covered her mouth. "I'm sorry. I'm—. Erik. I'm staring, right? I should stop."

"It doesn't help."

"You're like a god or something. You're not even human."

"Suddenly, the city seems too small."

"For you maybe."

"I should go."

Gemma was shining, too bright, too bright, so I looked straight ahead, up Tenth Avenue, or wherever we were standing. The buildings one after another, infinite.

"I'm sorry, Erik. I don't know what to say. I'm not sure I'm awake."

"You're still too much for me, Gemma."

"What are you talking about?"

"Too shiny."

"Now I know this is real. You're an idiot. Look at you, Erik. Unbelievable." She shook her head, and held on to her purse, almost hugging it. "I feel sorry for you. I'm serious. You're always going to be alone. You know that? No one's good enough for you. Nobody normal anyway. There aren't any goddesses left. I mean, there are, but not your size."

I don't know what came after this. Gemma disappeared, and I woke up somewhere else, some corner far from where I started. I couldn't do much more than wonder about you.

Are you a goddess seven feet tall waiting for her god? Or are you a girl who will know her husband when she sees him?

Inaction

I WENT TO BUY a gallon of milk and some cereal. How could I have been ready for what happened?

If you were to have asked me before this morning, "What did the man in the garage look like?" I would've been totally unable to answer. Tall, short, fat, thin? Blue eyes, brown, green, black? Bald? I don't know, I don't know. I only remember the garage and the window and the light; my broken arm; and I didn't have my belt.

I knew him. As soon as I saw him, one hand on his cart, scanning the cereal, only in profile, I knew him. I knew him. And you know what I did? Not a thing.

I had turned to concrete. I felt nothing for a moment, a long moment, as long as the life I've already lived. Then, he turned with his choice—Mini-Wheats, blue box, a splash of milk; I remember Mini-Wheats—and I saw his face. Maybe he's fifteen years older than me, hard to say, not much more. No sign of gray. No tiredness. The concrete melted, I found my skin, and all I could do, all I felt came to nothing more than a collapse.

Terror.

Thirteen years. I'm almost two and half times the height I was at five, fifty times as strong. I could have killed him with hardly any motion at all. Imagine everything I might have done to him, all the harm. Imagine the blood and broken bone.

Imagine him all chewed up.

Instead. Instead. Instead, instead, instead.

I did nothing. I let him pass. He hardly glanced at me. I was nothing to him.

I let him pass.

So I have to ask myself a question. What happened there? I was a little boy all over again, locked in a garage and helpless. No escape. Even when I recovered, even when I realized I was standing in the cereal aisle, even when I knew I could track him down in the store, knew I could hunt him and kill him, I did nothing. I let him go.

Am I a coward?

All this time I've been thinking I would be a hero. I had this idea I would save lives, give up my life willingly. But what did I learn this morning? I can't confront a criminal. I can't even go back in time and protect the boy I was, or punish the man who hurt him, hurt me.

Is there another answer? Quick, give me something before I break down completely. I'm enormous, I bleed, and the first time I can right a wrong, I turn into what?

Think, think.

I need an answer. Do you have one?

Maybe I'm not important enough to myself. Maybe once a victim always a victim. Maybe I'm not a vigilante. Maybe I don't have a thirst for vengeance.

Quarantine

FORTY DAYS. FORTY DAYS the flood covered the earth before Noah could open a window. How that ark must have smelled. Shit, urine, sex, death, rot, birth, blood, saliva, fear, rage, impatience. Salt. All the ocean. So much water.

Forty days and nights Moses spent on the mount without eating or drinking—no water—before receiving the laws on two tablets. We assume he must have been awake the whole time, begging God constantly for revelation. Maybe he slept. Or waited silently, ready to fill His order. He must have lost weight, around fifteen pounds. Twenty? A lean messenger.

Quarantine. I read somewhere, the word *quarantine* means forty days isolated. Meant to stop the spread of disease. Quarantine: an enforced isolation.

God enforced Christ's quarantine. What was His disease? The Son of Man endured the desert, tempted by Satan or Lucifer, propped up by angels, hungry.

Where will I serve my quarantine?

I need the park. I need trees, ferns, brush, and a public water fountain. My quarantine near home. I'll sleep outside.

Will I, like Christ Himself, come out of the wilderness hungry? Or will I eat myself? A knife—. I think I should go empty-handed.

◇

If I stare inward for forty days and nights, barely moving for hours at a time, what will I find? In me, what will I find in me? Or what will find me?

I'll write and write, still my greatest comfort—.

Wait. This is a fast, a deprivation. Deprivation before revelation, right? I must not bring pens and notebooks. I'll give up everything. I'll go empty-handed. I won't even bring you.

Response

LAST WEEK, I WATCHED a man kill a rat with a cinder block. He simply dropped the block on the rat. Not a sound, no squeal, no crack. Next, the bastard picked up the block and dropped it again. No blood, but the rat must have been killed. A crowd of kids, surrounding the fenced-in schoolyard, clinging to chain link, watching a murder. Nothing should die in a schoolyard, not even a rat.

This time, I acted. No agony. No fear. Action.

"Mister." I called over to the man. He held the rat by its tail, swinging it a little as he crossed the yard. "Hold up." I walked up to him and took his shoulder. That instant, his arm turned to wood. "Bury your victim," I said. "Up in the grass. One-handed. I'll stay with you until you're done."

"Why?" A stupid, stupid man to ask a question of a giant. How could he know whether or not I appreciate the taste of human flesh? Stupid but afraid: "I'm sorry."

"Bury the rat. Once you're done, I'm going to break off your useless hand to mark the grave."

And I did.

Salvation

I'VE GONE BACK TO the schoolyard every day for two weeks. Day after day, I walk around the fence. I don't expect to see anything other than kids yelling their heads off and running around like maniacs.

But I didn't expect to see a man kill a rat.

The city rat is our enemy, right? Ugly, sick, and vicious. That's what we think. Albino rats, those white lab rats, they're okay. They help us get to the bottom of our own brains. They help us sort out our diseases. These good rats go insane for us. They die for us.

City rats? They scavenge. They teach us nothing but fear. They make us angry.

I don't linger at the school. I don't pray. I walk around the outside of the yard to do nothing more than mark that spot where the rat died. *Ecce rat.*

Morbid? You think it's morbid?

I don't go to the schoolyard to brood about death. I go to remind myself of something I don't understand but find awful and sad.

You're right, though. It's time I give this up. Or make it into something more.

Quarantine.

My forty days in the park: who will witness me? Who will tell me to pick up and go? The police? A homeless man, a hermit?

What happens to a passerby who comes to the park to die and stumbles across me? *There*, the passerby will think, *but for the grace of God, go I.*

I imagine this. Days and nights in the park, fighting devils. Tiny demons, actually. They get caught in my hair and harass my eyes. I breathe them in, sneeze them out. They buzz my ears, like mosquitoes, and mine that vein running over the stone of my ankle. Then they lift away and vanish, but they've left their poison. I get sick. I throw up. I'm tired. Lord, how I'm tired.

All these days and nights to swat at demons. To listen for God, wait on God.

Imagine more. Halfway through, I can't say I've been tempted exactly, except by death. Suicide: the worst temptation. Satan's no fool. He doesn't even have to show up. The idea comes, inevitably, and twists up and comforts at the same time a sad person, or a person at wits' end.

Did Christ have to fight the will to die? How sad and angry He must have been. If He'd ended His life, though, more than one prophecy would have fallen down. He couldn't be allowed to die under the white sun and be buried in a wave of sand. But I could die. I could die and go unmissed.

My mother has Lincoln, so she wants for nothing. All they seem to do is hold on to each other and laugh. No. They walk. I don't even remember the last time I spoke to either of them alone without the other nearby. What do I do with this? I have both, or I have nothing.

The first week without food will be the worst. Headaches. Nausea. Delirium. Teaching the body to go without.

Fasting is an insult to the body. Proof of our will, right? Still, an insult.

Maybe I should sleep through it all. Hibernate—.

Impossible. Impossible and unwise. What if I sleep through the moment of my death?

Will I end my life in the park? No. No. I want to know why I've been put on this earth. What's a bloodletting? What's an everlasting flower? A never-ending cruciform? My mother whole? A wooden hand? Whatever else? All this speaks to my destiny, and I can't die before I know my purpose.

What will happen at the end of the fortieth day if I still don't have any insight into why I exist, why I suffer, why I'm hungry? What then?

Will I finally have you? Will you appear out of nowhere and lift me up and bring me home? Will you tell me I'm not a hero? Will you tell me to get cleaned up, go to college, and forget everything I've thought until now?

"Forget the miracles, Erik. I'm the only thing that's real."
You'll turn on the shower and hand me a towel. You'll take off
my clothes. "Love is real. There's nothing else."

"But what was the point?"

"Of what, honey?"

"Of any of it. The garage, my father's death, the headaches,
the miracles, the frustration, the loneliness. It can't have been
for nothing."

"No, not for nothing. But not for any one thing, either. By
the time you get out of the shower, your bleeding will be done
and everything healed. We'll get something to eat. You'll sleep.
Then you'll wake up and our life will begin."

THORN

I DON'T THINK I have a soul. It was beaten out of me. Maybe it's gone entirely. Or hovering, half alive, hovering close. Maybe it wants to come back. What if my soul wants to find a way back in? When it's safe.

◇

That must be painful, a soul returning home. More painful than dying. The sickness. The tearing apart. Ribs and chest. Lifting the heart, unlatching it to find the little case for the soul. That much pain and sickness. The fever. The infection. The blood. All to take back the one thing that will make me better. Make me human and good.

◇

This word: *omphalos*. Navel, belly button. In other words, the end of the umbilical. The center of us. All knotted up. No more womb food.

Is it possible to disappear into yourself through your belly button? Does light come through skin? Or is it complete darkness? Smell of blood? Something rotten?

◇

I think, think, think, but I can't figure anything out. The

167

holes in my brain. Something new inside of me, the Drillers.

I've lost chess to a hole in my mind. I can no longer play, and I barely remember how the pieces move. The queen in any direction, as far as she can or wants to go, and her use-less husband, the king, only one square, north, south, east, or west. It's the knight, armored and heavy. He can jump over anything and owes it all to his horse. I can't remember, how does he move? How many squares? An el?

◇

No job. No money. No school. No board games. No chess.

If I've forgotten how to play at war, does that mean I'm more peaceful?

◇

I saw a man kill a rat in a schoolyard. The schoolyard where I waited for Mala. Where a goat made of children crushed my finger under its hoof. My schoolyard. He crushed the thing with a cinder block. A rat. The man killed himself. Didn't he? A rat killing a rat.

That man was a kid once. He might have gone to that school, too. I don't know, but he went to school somewhere. He was a child, and then he grew up into a man that kills animals in a schoolyard. A self-hating rat. He was a boy once.

He dropped the block, and I had to walk away. I felt sorry

for the rat, and kind of sick, so I walked away. I couldn't stop thinking. It might as well have been a boy, a child, who killed the rat. I might've killed the rat. A killer of rats.

◇

Then, a raccoon killed in the street. Right in front of me. Its insides splashed over five feet of road. I saw it. The driver didn't stop. He must have known what he'd done. But this crime couldn't hold its own against the driver ten seconds later. His crime? He steered into the dead coon, crushing it. Blood on the tires.

Why would anyone do this? Hate. Rage. That's a man to loathe. A man who deserves to be thrown into a pit with hungry raccoons.

◇

I want to punish the second driver. I want to punish the man who killed the rat. I want to punish them all, the cruel and hateful. The liars. The cowards.

Go to the source.

Easy for me to say. All men and women start out as children.

◇

"Where is everybody?"

I felt empty. Almost dead.

"Nobody here but us." A Guardian laughed.

It all happened fast. Without my knowing.

"We slaughtered the others."

"What does that mean? Who's left?"

"We and our Sawmen. The Drillers."

"The Protector?"

"No."

"Why?"

"Just following orders."

"The Architect."

"As ever, the Architect lives."

"There's blood and shit all over the ground."

"War will do that."

◇

Something terrible and desperate, something brutal, crushes me from the inside. Stones. Laid on top of my heart and lungs. I can hardly breathe. The Architect, the Guardians, they have me under stones.

"The Architect will not kill you." The Guardian sets another stone. "Rather, he'll only kill you once."

Stone after stone after stone.

"Matters are resolving themselves quite nicely. Your mind crumbles little by little, a sandcastle at high tide, if you will." Another stone. "We break you down, saws, drills, and stones."

I'm cracking. Even so, I have to think it's less painful than if my soul were finding its way back in.

My soul: I'll never get it back.

"Why do you need your soul?" the Guardian spits. "There will only be longing and regret."

And some peace.

"It's too late for that."

What will I do after I'm dead?

"For a little while, you'll live."

ERIK AND THORN

I wake and feel the fell of dark, not day.

—Gerard Manley Hopkins

ERIK

THE HEADACHE WOKE HIM. It felt nothing like the weather headaches, the pressure of a devil's two invisible fists on his temples, when he could foretell rain or snow. Nothing like the headaches he got when he was a young boy that began, inexplicably, with the sound of a far-off train getting nearer and nearer, the pain that would strike him like a locomotive and land him in bed and make him cry. Nothing like the headaches he got when he grew inch on inch, month after month, when his bones creaked; or the headaches when his teachers or his friends yelled one thing and another at him.

"Erik, aren't you listening?"

"I won't tell you again, Erik, sit down."

"Over here, Erik. Over here, over here, over here."

This headache, all feathers and fire, woke him out of his sleep. It came with a voice.

"It's time to get up," said the voice of a thousand voices, a thousand men, women, and children. Even when it whispered, it roared.

"I'm awake." Erik spoke through his teeth and held his head in his hands. "I felt you before you spoke."

"Then rise."

Erik opened his eyes and saw the world as if he were an astronaut making the leap to hyperspace, when all the white stars stream by. Or as if he had woken in a blizzard, with the wind driving endless snowflakes. He couldn't keep his eyes open. Sick and frightened, he turned into the ground and crushed his face into the fir needles.

"I'm sick."

"Stand up," the voice said.

"And I think you've blinded me."

"I will guide you." The one voice of the thousand voices whispered and roared. "Erik, it's time to stand. Your quarantine is over."

Erik took a deep breath and got to his knees, then pushed himself up to his feet. He felt dizzy, and he wondered if he would throw up.

"Open your eyes," said the voice, "and the sickness will pass."

"I don't—"

"Obey me."

Erik opened his eyes. The stars and snow had slowed down. At last, the headache gone, he could see nothing but whiteness.

Somewhere close, a crow announced itself: *Caw caw; caw caw caw; caw caw.*

"Tell me your name," Erik said, listening for the trees, the wind, turning his head to where he imagined the crow perched.

"No name," the voice said, the thousand voices distilled to one. "Are you ready?"

"I have to be," Erik said. "Yes."

THORN

"THORN," THE ARCHITECT PURRED, "my son. Wake up."

Thorn lay still.

"You know very well you're alive." The Architect rocked back and forth in his chair, his hands clasped under his chin. "Open your eyes, son."

"I'm awake."

"Of course you are." The Architect folded his long hands in his lap. "Listen to me. Children, Thorn. Men and women come from children. You made this observation yourself."

"I came from a child."

"Torturers, rapists, liars, cheats, cowards. Your parents. Men with cinder blocks and cars and guns. These, too, every one of them, come from children."

"Tell me what you want me to do."

The Architect leaned forward. "Kill the children."

ERIK

"YOU'RE NOT BLIND, ERIK. Give yourself a minute."

"What's happening to me?"

"Your senses are combining, which is why you feel sick."

"What does that mean?"

"You're unifying. You're taking a step closer to eternal life."

"I'm dying?"

"You call it dying, Erik, but your death is not here."

"Unifying?"

"Yes," said the voice.

"I don't understand. I've never understood."

"No."

"I'm only eighteen," Erik said, "but my mind is older. And I'm tired."

"You're half a day from a long rest."

"I'm overwhelmed."

"I know."

"We have to go, though. I feel it. We have to go now."

"Yes."

"How do I walk?"

"You'll see in living things what look like small birds of light riffling their feathers. In the lifeless things you will see the birds asleep, their heads tucked under their wings. Motionless."

Erik moved his head around after his white eyes. The bright

birds fluttered or slept, and he took his first tentative steps. A different sort of blindness, but he picked his way over stones and the path of sleeping birds.

"Will you do me one favor?" Erik said.

"I may."

"Will you heal my wounds, stop the bleeding?"

"Yes."

The open skin on Erik's head, wrists, and feet closed. More than four years after it had begun, the bleeding stopped.

"Thank you," Erik said.

"You're welcome."

"Where are we going?"

"The place where you're needed."

"Is this place where I'll finally make sense of it all?"

"Yes."

THORN

"HAVE A PIECE OF toast for breakfast," the Architect urged. "Butter, peanut butter, jam, whatever you like."

"Salt."

"Salt, then. Juice?"

"Water."

"What else could a man just born, so serious, want more than bread, salt, and water?"

"Nothing."

"You're a thorn," said the Architect. "Prick fingers, imbed yourself in a palm."

"Spike an eye." Thorn swallowed salted toast. "There will be blood."

"Rivers and lakes, yes."

"How many? How long?"

"Until you get tired. Then turn the gun on yourself."

"My life will be short."

"Brief but devastating."

"I am a devastation. I have suffered to become a suffering."

ERIK

"HOW DID YOU FIND me?" Erik said.

"How can you ask that? Have you ever been out of our sight?"

"Who's the *our*?"

"All."

"Tell me."

"All."

"The All killed my father and made me bleed? The All gave me the headaches?"

"Trials to prepare you."

"And the miracles?"

"The entirety."

"The All is brutal." Erik spoke through his teeth.

"Some claim so."

"Where am I going? We're leaving the park. My quarantine's done."

"Follow me."

"Cars, people, the city streets. You'll keep me guessing until the end."

"You accepted the not-knowing."

"Not without frustration."

"You never really surrendered."

Silence.

"I won't ever meet her, my wife?"

"Not in this world."

"Which world, then?" Erik said. "I looked for her in this one. I waited my whole life in this one. You're crushing me. Which world?"

"The world of the All."

"Is that a promise?"

"Yes."

"Amen."

THORN

"SHAVE." THE ARCHITECT ROCKED. "Your hair, your beard, your entire body. Buy a package of ten razors. Any kind you want."

"Why?"

"Obey me."

It took a long time. Blood trickled out of cuts from head to toe. One slash in his ankle bled a long time. He left a red footprint on the bathroom floor.

"I haven't been this naked since I was a baby," Thorn said.

"Not even then. You were born hairy, a little ape."

"My mother told me that once." Thorn looked at himself in the bathroom mirror. "Blood." He swiped his hand across his throat. "Always blood. I'm surprised I have any left at all after everything. All my scars. Scratches, cigarettes and an iron, the bone through my arm, and so on."

"The other was hairy. You're smooth," the Architect said. "Now you're the twin of yourself. Your own brother."

ERIK

"WILL I BECOME AN angel?"

"The angels have already been decided."

"So, no."

"No."

"What then?"

"A saint."

THORN

"PRY THE DOOR," THE Architect said. "You're strong enough."

"Crowbar." Thorn spoke like the Guardians, gruff and low, commanding himself: "Use the crowbar."

He broke through the door.

"Excellent." The Architect smiled, so Thorn smiled. "Your whole life we've listened to this man on the other side of a wall play with his guns. Just look. You'll find them."

It took ten minutes to locate a large duffel bag and a black hard case in a bedroom closet. "Ah," the Architect said. "Unzip the bag."

Thorn did as told by the Architect.

"Treasure," the Architect sighed. "Leave the case, bring the duffel."

"What will I use?" Thorn said.

"Pistols."

ERIK

"RUN, ERIK. I'M LEADING you."

"I can run a long time," Erik said.

"Yes. We'll have just the right amount of time. Run two minutes, walk a minute, run two minutes, walk a minute. You'll need your breath."

"Where are we going? A fire? A crime scene? To stop something from happening?"

"Forward, Erik. Always forward."

THORN

"IT'S TIME I LOOKED through your eyes." The Architect stood up from his chair. "I want to see the world one last time."

Thorn had stowed the duffel of firearms in the trunk of the car. He drove. It would be a matter of minutes.

"I'm always surprised by the light. Somehow, you survive the light. Your eyes don't burn to ashes. Your skin doesn't burst into flame. But the brightness and heat. You, your kind, are miracles."

Right turn, straight, second left.

Stop sign.

"And the colors. Why so much, always so much? I prefer my monochrome, my purple, green, or blue."

Third left. Slow. School zone: 15 mph.

"And so, by and by, we're here. It's all nearly accomplished."

ERIK

"IT'S TIME I RETURN your sight."

Erik blinked in the sunlight and raised his hand to shield his eyes. "What's this?"

"The place you had to wait for."

"The schoolyard. I came here over and over. I saw a rat killed here not too long ago."

"Get your bearings and summon all your strength."

"Why?"

A car pulled up to the distant curb, beyond the yard and fence. The driver, a bald, thin man, stepped out and went around to the trunk.

ERIK AND THORN

Do not stop. Erik crossed the yard toward the car. *Behold. The enemy has arrived.*

Thorn opened the trunk and leaned in. He retrieved two pistols, loaded the clips the way he had learned online, and slid them under the waistband of his pants. When he shut the trunk and turned toward the school, he saw a giant coming toward him. Thirty, twenty, fifteen feet—.

"I never knew my purpose," Erik began, "until this very moment." He estimated the strength of the hairless man, about his age, standing ten feet away. Nothing to compare, half his size. Except the enemy seemed nearly as large with a gun in his hand.

"I never knew mine until this morning," Thorn said from behind the gun. He almost could not believe the size of the man opposite him: eight feet if an inch. Plaid shirt and jeans, a lumberjack, Paul Bunyan. But handsome, he admitted to himself, the handsomest man he'd ever seen. Young, like him.

"You really carved up your body," Erik said. "Blood everywhere, cuts and holes. Slow bleeding."

"And I see where the blood came out of your wrists and head." The Architect smirked, so Thorn smirked. "A martyr."

"You can see my scabs and wounds?"

"Look at you, man. How can you hide it?"

Erik ignored this. "I knew I'd die young," he said.

"Me too."

"Long as I can remember," Erik said, "I've had a thorn in my chest, a kind of frustration, a question."

"Here I am."

Erik grimaced and clenched his fists: "Neither of us will survive this."

"No." The Architect laughed, so Thorn laughed. "Though I'll last longer than you."

"I'm not so sure."

"Let the bullets decide."

"I have more than enough strength to kill you. You'll die, and it will all be finished. Both of us, over and done with."

"Hearts beat right to the end," Thorn said, and pulled the trigger.

The bullet did not stop Erik. The giant came and came.

AFTERMATH

One bleeding, one broken, a pistol between. Before anything else, before the sirens and police and panic, before the questions and guesswork, the boys lay at one end of a concrete yard, close together, a mess.

Three days later, the bodies long removed, the cleanup would end. Mid-morning, spring, but the sun a winter sun and white. And a river of children would pour through the door to reclaim their yard, desperate to play.

This novel would have come to nothing without good fortune and goodwill. My gratitude goes to my parents for their every help, and to my sister, the other side of a coin. To Sarah who, at seventeen, read and weighed in. To Madeleine. To Paige. To Alan Cumyn and Julie Larios. To Ana Deboo. To Martine Leavitt for her quick, deep kindness. To Michael Green. To my indulgent, honest agent, Brenda Bowen. To my editor, Jill Santopolo, keen and careful.

◇

If not for Michèle, her sudden arrival, I would have finally eaten myself alive. This book is for her.